THE INCREDIBLE DIARY OF...

North Yorkshire

Edited By Wendy Laws

First published in Great Britain in 2019 by:

Young Writers
Remus House
Coltsfoot Drive
Peterborough
PE2 9BF
Telephone: 01733 890066
Website: www.youngwriters.co.uk

Foreword

Dear Reader,

You will never guess what I did today! Shall I tell you? Some primary school pupils wrote some diary entries and I got to read them, and they were EXCELLENT!

They wrote them in school and sent them to us here at Young Writers. We'd given their teachers some bright and funky worksheets to fill in, and some fun and fabulous (and free) resources to help spark ideas and get inspiration flowing.

And it clearly worked because WOW!! I can't believe the adventures I've been reading about. Real people, make-believe people, dogs and unicorns, even objects like pencils all feature and these diaries all have one thing in common – they are JAM-PACKED with imagination!

We live and breathe creativity here at Young Writers – it gives us life! We want to pass our love of the written word onto the next generation and what better way to do that than to celebrate their writing by publishing it in a book!

It sets their work free from homework books and notepads and puts it where it deserves to be – OUT IN THE WORLD! Each awesome author in this book should be **super proud** of themselves, and now they've got proof of their imagination, their ideas and their creativity in black and white, to look back on in years to come!

Now that I've read all these diaries, I've somehow got to pick some winners! Oh my gosh it's going to be difficult to choose, but I'm going to have SO MUCH FUN doing it!

Bye!

Wendy

Contents

Ethan Brooklyn Mazfari (8) 90
Riley Watson (8) 92
Alfie Harrison (8) 94
Kaiden Craig Taylor (8) 96
Harriet Brocklesby-Brown (7) 98
Faye George (8) 100
Grace Proud (8) 102
Calvin Lewis McMahon (8) 104
Daisie Bennett (8) 106
Amelia Wilcock (7) 107
Keagan Lee Addison (7) 108
Kenzie Deej Mcpake (8) 109

Kestrel Class - Danesgate, York

Cayden Mayes (9) 110
Charlie Kilner-Marshall (9) 111

Nawton Community Primary School, Nawton

Isabella Freeman (11) 112
Alfie Blacklock (10) 115
Archie Welford (10) 116
Harrison Bryant (10) 118
Scarlett Bo Savic (10) 120
Megan Ryder (11) 122
Jess Blacklock (11) 124
Neve Kendall (10) 126
Jack Everett (10) 128
India Steele (11) 130
Annie Foster (10) 132
Jessica Hyde (10) 134
Ross Fahey (10) 136
Evie Dunsmore (10) 138
Faith Trinity Thatcher (9) 140
Grace Smith (9) 142

St Benedict's RC Primary School, Ampleforth

Kayah Scarlett Matuszewska (8) 143
Ellie Rose Makepeace (8) 144
Grace Humpleby (8) 146

Daisy Naylor Smith (9) 148
Ryan Kambli (8) 149
Isaac Raynar (8) 150
Ernest Jones (9) 151
Kaiden Daniel Baxter (9) 152
Amelia Jasmin Syms (7) 153
Lexi Hillier (8) 154
Albert Nichols (7) 155
Theodore Gabriel Carter (8) 156
Carlos Terricabras (9) 157

The Michael Syddall CE (A) Primary School, Catterick Village

Ella-May Chadwick (10) 158
Poppy Tallulah Levitt (10) 160
Libby Grace Sutherland (11) 162
Katie Proudlock (11) 164
Max Lewis Coates (10) 166
Keira Stokell (11) 168
Izabel Violet Painter (10) 170
Liam Martin (9) 172
Riley Lister (10) 174
Lauren Emily Freer (9) 176
Phoebe Barnard (10) 178
Francesca Rouse (10) 180
Lexie Hurst (10) 181
Lucy-Mai Fotheringham (10) 182
Jack Anthony Buttitta (11) 183
Stanton Sharkey (11) 184
Liam Townley (9) 185
Casey Ann Pickup (9) 186
Harry Hooson (10) 187
Justin Burgess (10) 188
Boe Kirk (10) 189
Lewis Bell (9) 190

Thomas Hinderwell Primary Academy, Scarborough

Chloe Gibson (9) 191
Kyle Charlie Smith (11) 192
Andreas Nikolos Neagoe (10) 194
Lily Sellers (11) 196

Daisy Grace Clayton (8)	198
Oliver Gough (7)	199
Mason Tindall (9)	200

The Diaries

A Crazy Day, But Sad

Dear Diary,

I am Lilly. I had just found out that my dad had died. He was the best. I ran away because I was so upset. I was crying for hours but then realised I didn't have the best reaction. Anyway, I ran to the woods, it was the closest place, it had a treehouse there.

I then went to the shop and bought some fairy lights, blankets, cushions and food and took them back to the treehouse and I decorated it. It was the best place ever for peace and I was happy that no one would bother me whilst in the treehouse and I could think and remember my Dad.

Chloe Halder (11)

Barlby Bridge Community Primary School, Barlby Bridge

A Day In The Life Of A Dog!

Monday
8:40am
Dear Diary,
This has been the worst day ever... My sister (Chloe) was annoying me so much. She kept on teasing me with my toy and not letting me have it. Meanwhile, Mum and Dad were getting ready for work. It took Mum ages and Dad like two minutes, Chloe was meant to be eating her breakfast but she wasn't.

Monday
9am
Dear Diary,
Chloe was finally eating her breakfast. Mum was just setting off and Dad just needs to take me for a walk before he goes to work. My sister had just gone to get dressed and me, well, I was chilling in the window. Dad said, "Come on Poppy, walkies." It was my time to have some fun.

Monday
9:10am
Dear Diary,
I got back from my walk and Chloe was at last ready for school and about to set off, but late as usual.
"Bye!" I barked to my sister as she went out of the door. Mum had gone and I was waiting for Dad to go so I could get some sleep.

Monday
10am
Dear Diary,
An hour had passed and I had got some sleep, no one was in. It was pretty boring so I went to eat some of my biscuits and have a drink, then, of course, go back to sleep till someone got home.

Monday
5pm
Dear Diary,
Everyone was home and I was having some playtime with Chloe. Mum and Dad were cooking tea, I was very happy about that.

Some time had passed and everyone was in bed and I went to sleep too. That was my day.
Bye for now but not forever,
Poppy.

Chloe Louise Thorpe (10)
Barlby Bridge Community Primary School, Barlby Bridge

The Incredible Diary Of... Fishstick

Dear Diary,

Hello, I've just had one of the worst days of my life. Should I tell you what happened? Yes.

I woke up, got dressed and went downstairs to eat my fish food and I felt a bit weird so I lay down and went to sleep. When I woke up, I was feeling better but I was late for school so I grabbed my bag and swam to school. School started at 9am and it was 9:50am.

I made it to school but I missed my favourite lesson which is PE and next we had a boring lesson, history. After history, we had English which is okay for me but the school bully was sitting next to me and I was starting to feel angry because he was calling me names like FT or Fries. Miss told him off and I ignored him so it was okay.

It was the end of school at exactly 3:15pm and I was happy because I had a dogfish (puppy) and I couldn't wait to see him. His name is Fish Bob and he is so cute. I found him in the pond next to mine which is Fish Pond 1 in Australia and I live in Fish Pond 2.

I burnt my dinner so I had to make another one. I had some fish food to eat. My dog ate a water snake which is good because there are tons of them around here and that was my day.

Alex Ropela (11)
Barlby Bridge Community Primary School, Barlby Bridge

The Incredible Diary Of... My Football Tournament

Dear Diary,

Today was the best day ever, well, most of it. First, we had a boring one hour drive to Leeds for a football tournament. We were against ten teams. The first eight matches were great until I tumbled over on my ankle and had to go off. We were winning 4-0 but there was a lead change.

After another five to ten minutes into the match, it became 5-4 to them. I wanted to get back on so I just ran. The game came to within thirty seconds left; I dribbled up and rainbow flicked it over someone, then someone from behind fouled me. The whistle went and I heard the word, "Penalty!"

"Yes!" I said.

There were ten seconds left so I placed the ball down, did my special move, known as the Cristiano Ronaldo move and shot. Guess what? I scored top bins. All my team piled on top of me, I was so proud.

After that, it came to penalties because we drew. We had to nominate five people and a goalkeeper. I was nominated, also Jack Green, Reece Elliot and Liam. Our goalkeeper was a big furious beast in the net - we were definitely going to win.

It was now down to one more penalty for each team. It was 4-3 to us, if I scored this we'd win no matter what. I scored and we won, told you we would!
We were in the final but be lost. My coach gave me a medal for Man of the Match.
Well, see you tomorrow.

India Taylor Clayton (11)
Barlby Bridge Community Primary School, Barlby Bridge

The Incredible Diary Of... Lily

Dear Diary,

My owner has left for work and I was alone in the house with the cat. I could hear him creeping down the stairs. How could he think he could eat his food without me? He entered the kitchen as I barged past him and cleanly devoured his food. You should have seen him shoot up the stairs, faster than a rocket I would say.

After I ate his food, I decided to entertain myself by throwing toys down the stairs and bringing them up again.

I was hungry again so I wandered around, looking for crumbs, when I came across a strange mechanism collapsed to the ground and it started ticking louder than before. I stared at the strange symbols that were decorated inside, then I realised it was telling me something. It gently told me something. The glass door and the cupboard door rattled strangely so I decided to leave it alone...

You know when I told you that I would leave the cupboard and the glass door open, right? Well, curiosity got the better of me. As the cupboard rattled I was able to open it. Some people may say curiosity killed the cat, which is a pretty reasonable thing to say as cats always fall off wardrobes.

Anyway, a bag of cat nibbles fell out, spilling everywhere as the back door swung open, spitting air into the living room. At the same time, the front door opened and my owner stumbled in.
It was a crazy day and everything was right after all, well I still left all the cat food on the floor.

Tymek Skubis (11)
Barlby Bridge Community Primary School, Barlby Bridge

The Incredible Diary Of... Hope, The Hybrid Person

Dear Diary,

Today, was my first day of high school. I couldn't wait to know what my transformation was! Locksworth High is not far from my house. I found my class and introduced myself.

"Hello, my name is Hope Bradford, I like drawing and I hope we will be friends. That's all."

The teacher (Mr Shens) asked who would give me a tour of the school. A ginger-haired girl volunteered. I couldn't wait.

Class ended. As I was exiting the room, that girl rushed up to me.

"Hi, I'm August, August Black," she told me, "I'm here to give you the school tour."

Going up the stairs, we started.

"These are the girls' changing rooms..."

After the tour, we headed for transformation class. This was a partner class so you had to choose a partner to attend the class with you. I chose August. The teacher (Ms McLegon) told August to transform. She asked how she did it.

"It's simple," she told her proudly, "you just think of something happy."

August succeeded and bear ears and little yellow wings popped out.

"I'm an angel honey bear!" she said excitedly.

"That's rare."

"Now, it's your turn, Hope."

After a moment, fox ears shot out, white swan wings and a bushy wolf tail. The teacher glared at me and said that I was a hybrid person, one of the last hybrid people alive. I am a swan crossed with a fox!

Adios!

Bianka Beloniak (10)

Barlby Bridge Community Primary School, Barlby Bridge

The Incredible Diary Of...

Dear Diary,

My name is Ashton. I live with my mother and brother. When I turned ten, I went on my Pokémon adventure. My partner was Charmander.

Something wasn't right. I needed a friend. I got my friends from school, Logan and Lucas. It took us so long but we finally got to Pewter City! I got to meet the rock type gym leader, Brock. He had some tough Pokémon but it was easy! So the first gym was gone and I got the boulder badge. The next gym was in Cerulean City and it was a water type. *Dun, dun, dunnn.* I was defeated at first but when I levelled up my Pokémon, victory was mine! I caught a Geodude on the way to the next gym!

Just then, Charmander started to glow. It was evolving! It evolved into Charmeleon, the fire-lizard Pokémon. So was Squirtle into Wartortle! I had a thunderstone to turn Pikachu into Raichu.

Twenty days later, when I had battled every single trainer and captured 151 Pokémon, it was time to battle the champion. I didn't believe it at first. It was Tyler, my little brother! He was very tough but I managed! Now that I am champion it was time to catch Mewtwo. I caught it with a Master Ball!

Ashton Firth (7)

Braeburn Primary & Nursery Academy, Scarborough

The Incredible Diary Of... The Lonely Fish

Dear Diary,

Well, I can't make an entrance so this will have to do. As you know, I'm a lonely fish, which is sad because you're probably reading this with a friend, my only friends are plastic coral. Sad times. Anyway, you're probably wondering why I am writing, it's because my bestie (now ex-bestie) has made me 100% jelly-jealous as you weirdos say it. I know you probably think, *how can fish be jealous?* Well, when they get replaced that's when they get jealous. I'll tell you how it happened...

I am a fairground fish and a girl called Emma won me and took me home to her mansion. She was weird, like super weird; she always wore rubber gloves and kept on cleaning my glass. She never left her room and her parents had to bring her meals. Emma sprayed her food with disinfectant twice and then ate it. Ew! Ew! Ew!

I don't know or care whether I told you but well I have two things: A... I'm a weird fish (I know what you're thinking) and B... I was claimed on Saturday. You know my ex-bestie, Nemo? Well, she picked him and got me and wasn't pleased.

Her mum came into her room and asked her how I was doing, you won't believe what she said!

She groaned, "I hate it! I don't want it! I wanted Nemo!"

I just swam to look out of the window.

Later on, she'd finally left her room and went to her gran's, which is next door.

While she was at her old, frail gran's, her mum snuck into her room like she had a secret plan, grabbed my bowl and drove me, yes, in a car to the fairground, went to where I came from (the salesman was on his break) and swapped me for Nemo!

The hatred in my eyes nearly made me blow up. I was furious. But, worst of all, every single fish jumped out of the tank into the hook-a-duck because I was there and I was different.

So, I'm here now feeling all alone and depressed. I don't even feel I can ever write again after this traumatising experience so this is the end.

I will miss you,

Bubbles.

Amber Clarke (11)

Braeburn Primary & Nursery Academy, Scarborough

The Incredible Diary Of... Santa's Workshop

An extract

Dear Diary,

The craziest thing happened last month. It all started when me, Lucy, and my older sister, Emily, were sat in our bedroom enjoying our lunch. Emily asked if I wanted to go to town. I said yes because I had some money from my grandmother. It was Christmas Eve so I got some last minute gifts for my family and friends. We were on the bus home when it all got odd. This bus didn't take us home. We didn't think much at first so we fell asleep. When I woke up, I looked out of the window to my left.

"We're in the air!" I yelped.

We were over solid blue ice, flying over the wonderful world. It was an experience I'd never forget. We landed on a beautiful sheet of ice. We were at the North Pole! I asked my sister if we would see Santa but she said I was being silly. She told me that there was no such thing as Santa so I shouldn't get excited! I told Emsy (which is what I call her sometimes) she was wrong and he *is* real but she rolled her eyes. Me and Emily went walking around and I spotted something out of the corner of my eye in the snow. I told Emily so she went

over to see what it was because I was petrified.
Emily yelped, "It's an elf!"
I went over to see what was going on and it
was an elf! I asked him if we could see Santa and
he said, "Do you believe in him?"
Of course I said yes! He led us down a large, dark,
gloomy tunnel until... there he was. Santa was
right in front of my eyes!
"Ahh, I've been expecting you two," he told me and
Emily, "how would you like to work for me?"...

Lucy Swift (10)

Braeburn Primary & Nursery Academy, Scarborough

The Incredible Diary Of...

Dear Diary,

My name is Olivia and you are going to be surprised because you will not believe what happened to me yesterday! It was amazing, incredible and exciting! I went to Scarborough Sealife Centre with my big brother, Jack, and my lovely cousins, Jaiden and Jude. We started looking at the spotty red and blue fish that were swimming happily in their tank. Suddenly, we all started to feel a little bit strange! Then my big brother, my cousins and me turned into big and grey, friendly sharks! We were in a small shark tank. The shark tank was not big enough. It could only fit four sharks in! We had been naughty and for a few minutes, we felt heartless, sad and petrified. Jaiden wanted to say, "I know all of us will be sharks for the rest of our lives!"

Then at bedtime, we slept all night.

The next morning we had some yummy, big, silverfish! As silver as a silver coin. Then some strangers looked at us. We played a game of who could be quiet for the longest. Jude and I won because we were quiet for the longest! Later we found a new friend called Jerry the shark. He looked scary but he kept us awake all night! None of us got any sleep.

I felt bored and nervous. All of us swam in our tank which made us feel better and comfy. We all had a conversation when Jerry got put in our tank. Then we had more silverfish for tea. We got to have a little swim which got all the dirt off us! We got in our beds. I had a dream about racing and I was in my bed! It was a crazy dream about sharks!

Olivia Ketteringham (8)
Braeburn Primary & Nursery Academy, Scarborough

The Incredible Diary Of...

Dear Diary,

My name is Lexy and you would not believe what happened to me today! I will tell you where it started which was in my bedroom where all my dreams come true! It is very cosy in here because it has pink and purple wallpaper and a blue cover on my bed and black pillows. I was with Lilly, Milly, Luke, John and my cousin. What happened today was that I became a princess!

Milly woke me up and said, "Wake up, princess!"

I got dressed and went downstairs and somebody said, "Ah, Lexy! How are you today?"

I replied, "Good, and you, King John?"

The king replied, "Great! And how do you feel today?"

I replied, "I had a nice and peaceful dream!"

Then all of a sudden, Luke came in and said, "Wake up from your beauty sleep! Well, you don't look very beautiful!"

He started to laugh. So did his girlfriend because he wanted her to. I shouted at Luke's girlfriend. "Have you seen what he is trying to do to you? He wants to use you to be popular!"

She told Luke that I was right. Then Luke told me he was sorry and then me, Prince Luke, Milly and one of my friends did skipping! When I went back inside, I found a portal in the forest and came back home! That was what happened to me. It was amazing but at least I found the portal otherwise I would still be stuck there! Hopefully I go on a more crazy adventure than this one. Well, time to go to bed. See you tomorrow, Diary! Peace out.

Lexy Ebejer (7)
Braeburn Primary & Nursery Academy, Scarborough

The Incredible Diary Of... The Young Scotsman

An extract

Dear Diary,

I am so annoyed! Why does everything bad have to happen to me? You're probably thinking, *what are you talking about?* Well, here you go...

I was sitting in my natural habitat (on the couch eating Doritos and watching TV) when something disturbed me. I knew who it was. I slowly turned my head. I was right. It was my mum.

She asked me. "It's such a nice day, do you want to go to the shop?"

If you don't know what that translates to, Diary, then here you go: "You're really lazy so get off your bottom and come to the shops!"

After preparing myself for the wilderness, I opened the door. I felt like Bear Grylls going on yet another adventure.

Many seconds later, I realised that my mum was walking a different route. Then I saw something, something mystical. I had never seen anything like it before (well, only in books). It was an ancient, beautiful cherry blossom tree! I stopped in my steps to admire it. I may have admired the tree for too long because when I snapped back into reality, my mum was halfway down the path.

After catching up with my mum, I was thinking that since my mum had dragged me out of the house, I should get something in return. I was thinking of something like a giant, luxurious chocolate bar, a million multicoloured gummy bears (not actually a million) or even a fizzy drink.

After browsing every aisle, I saw something, a fridge. There was one last bottle of Irn-Bru left...

Kiera Green (10)
Braeburn Primary & Nursery Academy, Scarborough

The Incredible Diary Of... Candy Land

Dear Diary,

"It's time to go to Candy Land!"

Down came my magical unicorn, who is amazing, and he took me up into the candyfloss clouds. In the distance, there was a dark chocolate castle jumping from candyfloss cloud to candyfloss cloud, all different colours. Then I noticed I was heading to the dark chocolate castle.

As the unicorn flew me around the castle to explore. I saw little munchkins making candy. There was a wicked witch shouting at the little people with her *booming* voice, shouting, "More candy! Get working!"

Then me and the unicorn decided to swoop down to save the little people so we told them to grab onto the unicorn's rainbow tail and hold each other's hands. Then we whooshed into the clear sky but as we looked back, the wicked witch was chasing us on a dark chocolate broomstick. Me and the unicorn decided to go closer to the sun so the dark chocolate broomstick started to melt! All of a sudden, she landed on the candyfloss clouds and something magical happened... She turned into the most beautiful princess you could imagine!

24

And for the happiness of lifting the spell, she granted us with one wish! My wish was to help the little people turn back into normal-sized humans and to return home, then with a bright white flash, we all returned to the town. The princess turned out to be my mother who had been lost for many years! We all had a huge celebration and all lived happily ever after.

Salise Esme Chapman (11)

Braeburn Primary & Nursery Academy, Scarborough

The Incredible Mr Irn-Bru

Dear Diary,

Today has been crazy. There has been absolutely horrible things and also amazing ones, let me tell you all about it.

Basically, I was at home with my mum, Debbie and Dad, Swayze and my brother, Charlie and don't forget my little cat, Ninja. We live in one of the smaller houses in Scotsman's Lane. We live on the north side, most people decide to live on the south side, that's where all the good jobs are.

We were at home when we heard a shrill noise. There was a huge hand inching into our home (which is literally a cardboard box). The hand reached in and picked me up.

My mum was clapping and shouting, "You'll enjoy it!"

My dad looked at my horrified face and smiled, "You're the chosen one."

The next thing I knew, I was in a new house? But I was moving, moving and shaking. I looked behind me to see a sticker. The sticker read: *Glasgow Irn-Bru Festival*. A festival means a party, right? *Well, that's amazing*, I thought to myself.

I decided to lie down and have a nap, so I could have enough energy for when I was there... When I woke up, I was being taken into a huge room. In the room, I saw... humans, huge fridges and humongous Irn-Bru posters. I got picked up and taken into a small room. A large, wide man stumbled through the door and started to spin my... head! He started to spin my head like a helicopter!

Zac Scholey (11)
Braeburn Primary & Nursery Academy, Scarborough

The Amazing Adventures Of The Shabby Shoes

Dear Diary,

I feel like a piece of rubbish, literally!

I was just polishing my tumultuous, lilac, purple, water-resistant laces when speckles of light dotted round my size 3 shoebox. I instantly knew it was time, time to shine and dazzle with my magnificent rose-gold tick. The susurration of workers was annoying me like crazy, because of their dumb voices ringing through my ears.

Finally, the metal barriers were opening their eyes, I couldn't wait. The crowds of people, okay, there were about six, burst in through the shop's automatic doors.

A couple of hours later, I saw the most glamorous (not as glamorous as me) lady stroll through the doors. I instantly knew it was destiny for me to join her. As I said ('cause I'm never wrong) she obviously chose me; however, as we nearly arrived at the counter, her crystal eyes seemed to have gotten glued to Cathie (my friend). It was almost as if she was a symphony to the woman's eyes. She dropped me and grabbed Cathie's box, leaving me on the wet, dirty floor until a weird worker put me back in my box - the wrong way.

Several minutes later, an eleven-year-old grabbed me, paid for me and put me on (who could resist?). But then the odour came - ewww - it was like blue cheese, mouldy milk and fish all blended together! Then, whilst going round numerous shops, she scratched my Nike tick off. How could she do that?

Ellie Adele Cherry (11)
Braeburn Primary & Nursery Academy, Scarborough

The Incredible Diary Of... Mr Carrot

Dear Diary,

Something happened today, you won't believe it so let me tell you.

After one week of being on that boring old shelf, someone picked me. *Wow, I'm going somewhere, this will be fun,* I thought. When she put me into the basket I met lots of new friends. We discussed going on so many adventures together. When we discussed where to go we thought of the same idea which was to the... carrot field.

We were so excited to go, but we realised that we were already in the boot of a car so we'd just have to wait and see where we will end up.

After ten minutes, we stopped. I could only make out a few words: 'Carrots are for tea tonight'.

We started to panic, the boot opened. She picked us up and into the house, through the hall and into the kitchen. She put us all into a cupboard.

After hearing we were there for tea it made me think, *when she opens the cupboard we won't be here.*

"Listen to this. If we all push on this wall we can get into a small pipe that leads to the roof."

30

After pushing on the wall for fifteen seconds it finally came through. All we had to now was climb up the pipe and we'd be free. One by one we climbed up, me first. I could feel fresh air when *bam!* It all went black and now I'm here alone hiding behind a clock on the wall.

Yours sincerely,

Mr Carrot.

Alfie Tayfun Roe (11)
Braeburn Primary & Nursery Academy, Scarborough

The Incredible Diary Of... Bob And Friends

21st January, 2007

Dear Diary,

Hi, my name is Bob and I'm an intergalactic alien. I'm from Uranus but sadly, while I was exploring space and enjoying the sights of the stars, my ship went into manual and I forgot to read the whole instructions booklet! After that, I crashed on, according to my radar, Earth - a very strange looking planet!

22nd January, 2007

Dear Diary,

It's my second day on this strange planet and guess what? I've learnt the people who live on 'Earth' give out free food in glorious silver cans. Also, today I met a young human girl called Mia. She is so kind and sweet. Guess what she said to me? "Arghh!"

I think that's 'You're gorgeous' in human-ish. Oh well! I guess I'm learning more and more about humans each day. Anyway, that's all for today!

23rd January, 2007

Dear Diary,

Day number three on planet Earth. My ship is still wrecked and nobody will help me. Maybe I'll ask that girl.

24th January, 2007

Dear Diary,

This is my fourth day on Earth. Wait, she is back for me! This time she brought another young girl called Emily. Guess what she said?

"Arghh!"

"Oh, thank you," I said back.

Then she ran away. I think she wanted to play alien tag.

What do you think I should do to fix my ship?

Goodbye for now.

Mia-Rose Elizabeth Walker (11)

Braeburn Primary & Nursery Academy, Scarborough

The Incredible Diary Of... Dorothy Gale

Dear Diary,

I've had the most incredible day of my life. I was in a mythical land. I heard a voice say, "You are in Munchkin Land. Now just call it Oz." I killed the Witch of the West and got to keep the ruby slippers!

I was walking along the yellow brick road when I met a talking scarecrow.

He said, "Please can you unscrew the nail that is holding me onto this wooden post?"

Since I am a kind girl, I helped him and he danced and sang in joy.

"Oh, thank you!" he cried out in laughter. We walked along together following the yellow brick road. We met a man made of tin. We couldn't understand him, but then the scarecrow could.

"Please put oil everywhere on me and take the vines off me. The person who made me forgot to put oil on me every day. He left me to be a rusty man!"

We followed the yellow brick road.

"Be careful, there are lions, tigers and bears here!"

On the road, we met a lion, so I hit him, then he started crying like a baby.

I said, "Oh, I'm sorry, I didn't want to hurt you."

Then the Wicked Witch appeared.

"Mwaha!" she screamed. "I've finally found you. Now give me your ruby slippers or your friends die!"

But I killed her by throwing water at her!

Skye Grace Noon (7)

Braeburn Primary & Nursery Academy, Scarborough

The Incredible Diary Of...

Dear Diary,

I'm Chase and you would not believe what happened to me today. It was a normal day at the beach with my friends playing football and my mom called us for tea.

When I got in, I said, "Shazam!" and turned into a superhero. So did my mom and my friends Coby, Rebecca, Thomas and Rhys. I am joking, my friends do not turn into superheroes. They turn into monsters! Coby turns into a T-rex, Rhys is the best robot Lamborghini, Thomas turns into a football champion robot and Rebecca turns into a unicorn. I can deactivate but when my mum turns into a Shazam woman, she doesn't know how to deactivate back into a human!

One hour later, a bomb set off!

"Oh my heavens, what's happening right now?"

"Let's go save the beach! Or do you want the whole world to collapse?" I shouted.

"That sounds terrifying!" replied Thomas.

"It is," I said. "What do you think?"

"Let's split up and go!" Rebecca said.

"Okay, but do you think we can do it?" Coby shouted.

"Just come on!" I said.

"Fine!"

We all went to Scarborough beach and used our superpowers to put the world back together! I clicked my fingers and then we were back to normal, just in time for tea.

Chase Carter Eade (8)

Braeburn Primary & Nursery Academy, Scarborough

The Incredible Diary Of... The ABF

Dear Diary,

Today, me and my crew (me, Alfie, Billy and Lincoln) went to an abandoned farm (an ABF for short) because one of Alfie's friends had suggested it to him. It was quite an adventurous journey to get there. It was also really exhausting but sort of worth it! There were lots of cool things like bike parts and even whole scooters and bikes!

It was about six o'clock (6:07pm to be exact) when we got there. An hour later, we got spotted but not by another explorer or the police, by a clown. A killer clown with a knife and red hair! He began to chase us. He started to sprint so we did too.

We constantly ran around the farm about three times trying to lose him but it didn't work. There was an entrance to the upstairs area so we made sure he wasn't able to see us and we went up there and he didn't know. There was a window that we kept looking out of to make sure he wasn't nearby.

We stayed up there for about ten minutes but then he came running up to our location and we just managed to jump out of the window and he jumped out too.

We guessed he'd hurt his ankle because he was a lot slower now. We then decided to run as far away as possible and luck struck because a police car drove by and arrested the clown! We were safe... for now...

Jay-Jay Richard Marshall (11)
Braeburn Primary & Nursery Academy, Scarborough

The Incredible Diary Of... The Glorious Glasses

Dear Diary,

You will never believe what happened to me today! It all started when I was sat comfortably on the shelf in Specsavers with my two friends Karlie and Emily. We were talking about how Maddie was bought by a very rich lady; she knew that we wanted to be bought. I mean, you would if you knew all the plans the other glasses had conjured up to escape. Anyway, back to it, we were gossiping when... a lady walked in. She strode straight towards us (I was extremely scared). She stared at me with her fiery emerald eyes and then she picked me up. It felt as if I was defying gravity until she slotted me onto her nose. But after much consideration, she put me back on the old, uncleaned shelf, where I've lived for the past four years!

After she'd left the shop, I sighed with relief when all of a sudden, another lady came in, she more-like stumbled through the door and she hobbled over near the till (where I am) and once again, she grabbed hold of my fragile legs, with her shaky hands, which I didn't feel safe with. And I was right about it as she dropped me (yep, let me fall to the ground).

I am now recovering from my fall, I'm just telling my friends. I've got to go now as a lady is coming - I need to hide!

Sophie Colley (11)
Braeburn Primary & Nursery Academy, Scarborough

The Incredible Diary Of...

Dear Diary,

I'm Brooke and I'm going to write something absolutely amazing in your wonderful pages. Today I was at Playdale Farm with my friend, Macie. She wanted to go to the soft play area but I wanted to go and see the animals. We went to Playdale Farm and we bumped into someone called Farmer Pete! He had a guinea pig called Billy and a donkey called Dylan. Then me and Macie skipped off to the barn. We stopped at a pen and there was a donkey in it and lots of guinea pigs scattering all over the fresh new hay! We went nearer and then started to stroke the donkey and one of the small guinea pigs. Then there was a flash of brightness! It stopped and me and Macie were baby donkeys! The donkey and the guinea pig had become little boys! One with blonde hair was the donkey and the one with brown hair was the guinea pig! They laughed at us and ran off to the gift shop. Me and Macie got into the pen, being careful not to stand on the guinea pigs. Soon the morning had passed and there was that brightness again! Me and Macie were now guinea pigs. We started to scramble out of the pen and go to the soft play area.

When we got there, we turned back to normal! When the boys went into the barn to check on us, they turned back into animals!

Brooke Lola Byerley (7)

Braeburn Primary & Nursery Academy, Scarborough

The Incredible Diary Of...

Dear Diary,

My name is Charlie and you would not believe what happened to me last week! I went to a smelly, cold and frightening zoo because my mum forced us to have a family day. I really didn't want to go! I wanted to play out but something amazing and unbelievable happened at the zoo. We looked around the zoo and we saw noisy, brightly coloured parrots, huge, black gorillas and some big, grey elephants. Next, we went to see the cheeky, brown monkeys that were swinging on the trees. That's when it happened. Suddenly, I was a cheeky, brown monkey swinging in a tree too! I felt sad, brave and upset. I was so scared that I wouldn't be able to get out of the monkey enclosure, but I had to be brave at the same time. I told myself I should *never* be frightened.

I decided that I wanted to have some fun so I started to swing on the trees with the other cheeky, brown monkeys. The cheeky monkeys stopped swinging on the big, brown trees and got off the tree and lay on the grass and had a very long sleep.

They slept through the light morning and the dark night and then while they were sleeping, I was still swinging on the tree all alone.

After that, when the other monkeys woke up, I went to sleep.

Charlie Randall (7)

Braeburn Primary & Nursery Academy, Scarborough

Confusing Future

Dear Diary,

Hi, my name is Macie and there is something weird that happened to me today and to my two friends, Brooke and Lilly. We were out for a walk and there was a portal right in front of us! We were on our phones so we did not see it and when we walked through it, we went to different places. Brooke was at McDonald's working, I was in a house and Lilly was out shopping. We didn't know where each other had gone so we started ringing each other to meet up in a second. When I came off the phone, I looked down and I looked taller. It was very confusing! It's like we had gone to the future. Suddenly, I heard a doorbell! It was Lilly and Brooke! They said they had been waiting an hour. I apologised, then we went to the park but it was not there! The rocks you're meant to jump on had dirt all over them. The park we played in was wood all over! The swings had fallen down. We were all confused so we went to the shop to get some ice cream to see if we gave ourselves brain freeze, it might refresh our memories. It did not work! We went to the field next to it and then a portal popped up!

We went through and we were back at the park! It was all back to normal. We were so happy we gave each other huge hugs.

Macie Prince (8)
Braeburn Primary & Nursery Academy, Scarborough

The Incredible Diary Of...

Dear Diary,

My name is Alfie and you would not believe what happened to me today! As soon as I got home from school, I asked my mum if I could go to the park with my friends.

When I got to the park, it was raining and it was dark. We were all soaked. Then there was a lightning strike right in front of us! Just then, the rain and dark became sun. It was like I controlled water! Next, my friends turned into an octopus and a shark! I suggested we get to the sea quickly. We lifted them into the blue, loud ocean and I found out I could breathe underwater. We went to the bottom of the black, rocky and scary, dark cave. It looked terrifying. Then a giant octopus came and trapped us in the cave. Then Emma the shark and William the octopus and I tried to break through. Then I suggested I could smash through it with my fist. I managed to break through and I had muscles. We swam off and we never saw the octopus again.

Just then, we saw a house. We thought we could live in it. We were watching movies on the couch and we heard a noise. We pressed a button. It was the security button because we had security.

Then, outside the house, there was a light. We investigated and it was a city...

Alfie Slaughter (8)
Braeburn Primary & Nursery Academy, Scarborough

The Incredible Diary Of... Mogo And Me

Dear Diary,

Today was amazing! I was playing hide-and-seek like my normal self. Then I decided to hide in the woods. Then I decided to go further into the woods, further than usual. Then I started to feel a cold chill on the back of my neck. I turned around to see a whole new world! It was as soft as a blanket. It was a winter wonderland! There were trees as tall as skyscrapers. It was so amazing!

All of a sudden, my amazement was interrupted by this strong human-wolf (yes, I know that sounds weird but that's the best way to describe it). I asked what its name was. He said he was called Mogo. I introduced myself and said how I'd ended up there. He told me I was in a place called Narnia and that I was special because I am a 'real human'.

Then, after we got to know each other, Mogo showed me around Narnia. I swear it was the most beautiful thing I've ever seen! Then we reached the castle. It wasn't any ordinary castle, it was the ice castle where the nasty queen who didn't like Christmas lived!

I was so amazed I didn't even realise Mogo had gone! I looked for Mogo all day. He was nowhere to be found.
I hope I find him tomorrow!

Paige Saltmer (11)
Braeburn Primary & Nursery Academy, Scarborough

The Craziest Day Of My Life!

Based on 'The Last Wild' by Piers Torday

Dear Diary,

Hi, my name is Kester Jaynes and I'm twelve, nearly thirteen and I have ginger hair. Today has been a crazy day because I woke up and ninety-nine grey pigeons and one white one were just sat there on my bed and my floor! I thought it was just a dream until I realised that what was actually happening was reality. I was shocked.

About five minutes later, a huge group of cockroaches came running into my bedroom. It was like I was being attacked or something! The pesky varmints told me that I needed to leave Spectrum Hall (my prison). Then suddenly, loads more cockroaches slid under my door, holding the fat warden's key card. I couldn't believe my eyes! They swiped the key card from outside of the door and opened it and told me that I needed to help them save the last wild. I didn't know what they were talking about but I was kind of worried.

We left the room, trying not to get caught by the CCTV cameras.

Out of nowhere, two huge moths flew onto the cameras so we wouldn't get caught! We then ran into the elevator (which the cockroaches called the big metal cage).

Gotta go Diary! I will tell you all the details another day.

Emily Bell-Lawrence (10)

Braeburn Primary & Nursery Academy, Scarborough

The Incredible Diary Of... Bella Danceson

Dear Diary,

You won't believe what happened. I am a very happy farmer. I'm caring. I was quite happy today. My goat was being sold to a farmer in Russia. He was here. The goat was bleating loudly in every direction possible. The farmer was saying thank you and paying me until...

"The ghost has got sunglasses!" exclaimed the farmer, shocked.

Then the goat spoke! "Dance battle!"

I said, "Okay!" I did hip-hop, the goat did some street dancing. I was exhausted. The white and brown goat won, I remembered my farm is called Danceson Farmyard. I felt a bit of sadness run through my nerves. I went for a walk, then a superhero called Thor came down with a thud. I said, "I am a farmer."

He said, "I am too!"

We went to the farmyard. "My goat had a dance battle, now I've sold it. It was called Dance-Arena-Roo!" Thor was a fantastic farmer. We got a hammerhead shark because Thor had a heavy hammer and lots more animals, such as Burt the pig, Rose the dog and Shelby Rose, a French bulldog, and much more!

Alice Marie Fawthrop (8)

Braeburn Primary & Nursery Academy, Scarborough

The Incredible Diary Of... Jodie

Dear Diary,

My name is Jodie and you will not believe what happened to me today! I have blonde hair and a spotty white and black top and fishtailed hair.

I went to the Sea Life Centre with my friend, Skye, and I saw some fish called Maria the whale and Emma the octopus.

Me and Skye drove down to the Sea Life Centre and got our passes out and gave them to the person at the desk. We got our picture taken and looked at the fish. Skye needed the toilet. I touched a picture of a shark and suddenly, I turned into a shark! I tried to talk and it worked so I went to a whale and said, "What is your name?"

"Maria the whale," she said.

"How do I get out of here?"

"Take a left, a right and a left, then go down the sewers and you'll pop out of your toilet at home and then you can turn back into a human."

I met a shark called Rebecca, she took me to the way out and on the way, I saw an octopus called Emma.

Finally, I got out, then Skye just went out the door. I just managed to catch her! That's what I did today.

Jodie Gill (8)

Braeburn Primary & Nursery Academy, Scarborough

The Incredible Diary Of... The Amazing As!

Dear Diary,

You won't believe what happened to me today. I was in the shops (as normal) just chilling on the shelf, when another can of mushy peas was put on the shelf. It was so exciting and unbelievable, I just hoped that people wouldn't come and pick the other can of mushy peas up. If somebody did I would be so depressed; then I would be the only can of mushy peas left.

I introduced myself to the can of mushy peas and asked what his name was and shockingly, I got the reply of Alfie, which was amazing because my name is Aimee and they both begin with an A. I was so happy, joyful and light-hearted. Alfie was amazing. I hoped we could be friends.

I took all my courage to ask Alfie if we could be friends. Before he answered, a stupid girl pushed him off the shelf and *splat!* Alfie was destroyed. I was miserable.

I hope that Alfie will remember me. I'm stood here right now crying with depression. I hate that girl who pushed him off the shelf. I can't handle Alfie being gone. Maybe I should push that girl over?

Aimee-May Lucy Sewell (11)

Braeburn Primary & Nursery Academy, Scarborough

The Incredible Diary Of...

Dear Diary,

My name is Lewis and I've had a crazy day. You will not believe it!

It was a sunny day so I went to the Sea Life Centre to see all the huge, small and cute sea creatures, which were in tanks as big as trucks. I have some animal friends called Cole the mole, Sail the whale and Sam the clam.

When I arrived, I noticed something strange. I decided to walk through to see what would happen. After I got in, I was in a tank with my friends Sail and Sam. I knew that the only way to escape was by asking my friend Cole to dig a hole so I could escape! I was quite confused in there and I was super nervous because my friend may not have come to save me. Luckily, Cole came to save me from the tank by digging a hole my size so I could get through it. But there was a problem getting out of the Sea Life Centre, I had to go through the parking lot.

After we'd escaped, no one was hurt and everyone was safe, then I drove to my warm, cosy, comfortable house. I can't believe my day!

Lewis Ramsden (8)

Braeburn Primary & Nursery Academy, Scarborough

The Day At Mini Monsters

Dear Diary,

My name is Whitney and you will not believe what happened to me today. It was like my worst nightmare! I was scared because I went to Mini Monsters and turned into a monster! I went to play and when I ran past a monster, I turned into one! When I turned into a monster, all my friends did too! We quickly signed out of Mini Monsters and went outside so we could be us again! But it turned out it was just a dream so I woke up.

I said to my aunty that I'd had a dream about turning into a monster.

My aunty said, "No!"

When I got to school, I told Summer, Lilly, Macey and Brooke. They all said that was their dream too!

I said, "Remember we are meant to be going to Mini Monsters today as well because it is my birthday!"

"Why are you so scared about it?" Summer said.

"Well, what if our dreams come true?"

"They won't, don't be silly. It was only a dream!" Summer said.

Lilly said, "Ha ha!"

Whitney Hudson (8)

Braeburn Primary & Nursery Academy, Scarborough

The Incredible Diary Of... A Pencil

Dear Diary,

Oh, Diary! Oh no! Help me! The most tragic and most mesmerising, gobsmacking, unbelievable and confusing things (and yes I mean things) have happened to me today. And yes, as I said before, I haven't been living on the moon today and trust me on that one. Let me explain...

It all started today when I was dreaming away in my cosy little bed called Shelfy, when somebody picked me up and I'm not kidding, I actually got picked up, but let's get over that and talk about the main stuff, they disturbed my beauty sleep. You know like I'm not the only one who needs sleep, humans and only humans.

I then got chucked on the floor like I was a piece of stupid old rubbish. That is very nice (not). I still can't get over it, it is sooo much of a big deal, but I can't keep chatting to you, I need to go to the main problem. I need your help and I need it fast. So can you? Will you? Please!

Bye Diary, a dog is about to munch me up.

"Argh!"

Carli Ireland (11)
Braeburn Primary & Nursery Academy, Scarborough

61

The Incredible Diary Of... The Super Cuber

Dear Diary,

You will not believe what happened to me today. It's unbelievable.

I smashed the world record time for the three by three, which is a Rubik's cube, which is a puzzle. I did it in 2.45 seconds. Yes, I did it that fast. It was like nothing. Well, I did practise. Well practise does make perfect. That's how I got to be the fastest of all time.

Guess what happened? I got powers. Yes, real powers! It all happened when I was doing an experiment. I mixed two chemicals together then *poof!* The chemicals fell on me and I looked at my feet and I seemed to be floating, I was flying, yes flying.

Suddenly extraterrestrials approached Planet Earth, our planet in the Milky Way. They came from the Goldilocks Zone to destroy Planet Earth which has seven billion humans on it. I decided to use my powers to save Planet Earth and save the day.

I was worrying, not knowing what would happen to Earth.

Anyway, goodnight.

Pierre Henry Fernand Pihan-Silcock (11)

Braeburn Primary & Nursery Academy, Scarborough

The Incredible Diary Of... The Girl With The Red Scarf

Dear Diary,

I found a red scarf, it was as red and as soft as a teddy, but it was hanging off an old, rotting tree. When I put it on, I felt a little tingle.

When I went back home, I saw a boy.

He said, "Hello, girl in the red scarf."

When I got back home, there was a mirror in my bedroom. I told my mum about it.

She said, "Well, how did it get there?"

I looked in the mirror, a face appeared!

It said, "Make a wish." I was so scared.

I said, "I want to be rich."

When I woke up the next morning, I was in a posh bed. When I went downstairs, there was a posh table with a posh breakfast. I took my scarf off and put it on the chair, then it went pitch-black and a witch appeared! She waved her wand at me so I quickly put my scarf on, then I was back home in the kitchen, at the table. I quickly ran upstairs into my bedroom, the mirror was gone, so was the scarf.

Demi-Jade Shepherd (8)

Braeburn Primary & Nursery Academy, Scarborough

The Adventure Of The Twins

Dear Diary,

Yesterday was incredibly exhausting! The day started like any other. I was there looking after my baby twin girls.

At night, I was tucking them into bed. I was just going to bed myself and I heard a noise downstairs. It sounded like *bang! Clang! Smash!* I checked downstairs and no one was there. I went upstairs to check on the twins and they were *gone!* Me and the rest of the family went on a quest. Just before we were about to find them, there was a note on the door. It was a clue so we worked out what the clue said and made our way to the destination. We discovered another clue and it went on and on. We were just going around in circles but we must have not read the clue properly. We were foolish and didn't check the back of it, so now it made more sense so this was the final clue. It took us to the crying twins. After an amazing adventure, at least we got the twins back. Bye for now.

Lillie Ramsden (11)
Braeburn Primary & Nursery Academy, Scarborough

The Incredible Diary Of... A Teddy On A Shelf

Dear Diary,

I was sleeping when something woke me up by picking me up. When I opened my eyes I saw a beautiful little girl who was beneath me. She smiled at me. Her mum (who was called Beth) picked me up from the shelf and gave me to her. They carried me to a thing called a till.

When we left, she was hugging me all the way to her house where she put me on a thing called a bed, where there was another teddy.

"Hi, my name's Tom, what's yours?"

"Hello, my name's Pipi."

The girl came in and she said, "It's alright, I know that teddies are alive."

After that, she told me it was time for her bath, then Tom and I talked for a while.

The girl came in and said, "It is time for bed," with excitement.

She couldn't wait to cuddle me all night or even longer.

Goodnight Diary, see you tomorrow, Pipi.

Summer Lea Monks (10)

Braeburn Primary & Nursery Academy, Scarborough

Is The End Near Or Not?

Dear Diary,

Today was horrific! I went out with Billy, Alfie and Hayden and we went to an abandoned farm. Hayden kicked down the door. I saw a figure at the end of the corridor. First I thought it was a mannequin, so we carried on walking down the corridor. Alfie entered the loft. He saw some mannequins and he fell with a thump. He told us about the mannequin. We heard something looking down the ladder. I looked at the top of the ladder and saw the mannequin. We ran to the exit but the door closed. We went the other way and climbed up the ladder. We had to be brave so we all jumped out of the window at the same time. We were hurt but we carried on running. We ran to the closest place possible - the school. He had a chainsaw! We ran to the caretaker, Mr Jordan. We told him about the problem so he called the police. So far, we don't know if he is still in the world of freedom.

Rikki-Jay Arnold William Allison (11)

Braeburn Primary & Nursery Academy, Scarborough

The Incredible Diary Of...

Dear Diary,

My name is Rebecca, you will not guess what happened today! It was amazing, exciting and mind-blowing. I was at the zoo in Flamingo Land with Jodie and my cat called Pepsi. My mum and dad came too. We looked around the huge park, looking at all the different animals. There were pink flamingoes, fluffy lions and stripy tigers. Then we went to see my favourite animal: the cheetah. My mum, dad, me, Jodie and my cat, Pepsi, walked slowly and stroked the cheetah! That's when we turned into cheetahs! But Pepsi didn't turn into a cheetah so we had to try to turn back into humans. We felt upset.

Finally, we had to make a machine to make us humans again. We ran home and had tea and cupcakes. It was amazing. I had a shower and cleaned my hair, then we went shopping, it was amazing.

Rebecca Joyce Stone (8)

Braeburn Primary & Nursery Academy, Scarborough

The Incredible Diary Of... The Sleeping Packet Of Crisps!

Dear Diary,

You won't believe what happened to me today, just to give you a clue, I'm writing this in someone's stomach.

Earlier today, I was having my all day sleep when I was rudely woken up by a noise grinding in my head, it was the family waking up, the human family.

I was so annoyed, why do they always wake me up when I'm trying to get some rest. I went back to sleep after the family went out and when they got back I think you know what happened. I was woken up by another noise. Can't I get *any* sleep around here? I went back to sleep again after that. In the middle of the night, I heard a strange noise, someone had broken in! After a few seconds, I realised it was the family! Wait, what are they doing? "Ow, my head, argh!"

Henry Hagan (11)
Braeburn Primary & Nursery Academy, Scarborough

The Incredible Diary Of...

Dear Diary,

My name is Rhys. Today I went to the zoo. I took Roy the magical pig and Treacle, my pet bearded dragon. Today we went to see the dinosaurs, but Roy fell in the water so I quickly got my camouflage diving suit on and saved him while Treacle licked the dino's eyes out! Suddenly, I remembered Roy had booster ears so we hovered out of the zoo. Then we all shrank to the size of a spider! Then we teleported to prison and then grew to our normal sizes. We were stuck for half an hour, but then Roy needed a poop so we got out. I threw grenades at the guard so we would definitely get out safely. Then we met an alien called Bob, who let us ride his UFO for an hour. We went back home and jumped down the chimney. We landed on the sofa and watched 'Uncle Grandpa'.

Rhys Sellers (7)

Braeburn Primary & Nursery Academy, Scarborough

The Incredible Diary Of...

Dear Diary,

My name is Skye and you will be shocked! I went to the Sea Life Centre and suddenly, I turned into a shark and I was shocked, scared and worried. I was in a tank with a shark called Happy and a turtle called Smelly. I was so worried but the turtle called Smelly told me that if I could escape from the tank, I would turn back into a person! I knew it would be tricky to get out of the tank but I had Happy and Smelly to help me. We started creating a plan to help me but now I had to turn back into a person. I had to kick myself, and then I would turn back into myself. Now I don't need to stay awake all night and I can lie down in bed and go to sleep.

Skye Hall (8)
Braeburn Primary & Nursery Academy, Scarborough

The Incredible Diary Of...

Dear Diary,

My name is Jasmynn and you would not believe what happened today! I met some friends and they were animals and they were a little bit weird but Thomas was a chicken and I was a magical princess. This all happened while I was watching Netflix on television. Suddenly, a brown, feathery wise owl flew out towards me. He flapped his wings and I was a pretty princess. Thomas was a fluffy chicken but we had been transported to the middle of Center Parcs.

In Center Parcs, the owl's helper was Tiny the turtle. Thomas threw a football at the owl. Then we went to go and get some hot chocolate because it was freezing.

Jasmynn Parkin (7)

Braeburn Primary & Nursery Academy, Scarborough

The Incredible Diary Of... A Queen Of Hearts Dress

Dear Diary,

Today, I was nice and comfy on my pole and then you won't believe what happened to me. I was tried on by a posh girl willing to buy me and wear me all the time! But then her mother said, "No, go more classy like blue or black, not rose-red!" I was sad and in despair.

After an hour, she came back and bought me! I was then worn at a wedding and she went to a party with me. She went everywhere with me! I love my new owner. I'm sure she'll wear me every day. She is the best owner in the world!

Stacey Brooke (11)

Braeburn Primary & Nursery Academy, Scarborough

The Incredible Diary Of...

Dear Diary,

My name is James and you will not believe what happened today! It started in my green, cosy and nice bedroom with my amazing friends, Lewis, Charlie and Thomas. I was going to the shops when I turned into a big, humongous husky dog! I was going to the park but everyone was scared of me! I was really big and tall, everyone was terrified of me because I was scary! It was terrifying. I was really scared. I was black, grey and white and had a bit of brown. I was fluffy. Now I'll be a husky dog forever!

James McNeill (7)

Braeburn Primary & Nursery Academy, Scarborough

The Incredible Diary Of... Sophie

Dear Diary,

I baked a lovely, beautiful, delicious cake. I didn't want to take it on the bus. I thought it would spill. I would feel very sad and angry. Then the bus stopped and it splattered onto my dress! I screamed the bus down. It was so wonderful to get off the bus! I never want to go on a bus ever again, but my journey is far.

Sophie Marie Lister (8)
Braeburn Primary & Nursery Academy, Scarborough

The Incredible Diary Of... The Worst And Best Day Of My Life

Dear Diary,

Last week, I scored a hat trick against Wolves in the UEFA Champion's League semi-final to make the scoreline 3-0 to Leeds United.

Today was the day I had dreamed about my whole life - the UEFA Champion's League *Final!* It was amazing, the crowds were cheering for us to go on and win the cup.

After two seconds, I took a shot from the halfway line. It hit the underside of the crossbar and then ricocheted in. After that glorious goal, the crowds were roaring.

Thirty seconds later, I had a penalty to take. I was so excited! I lined up the ball and took three deep breaths before kicking the ball in the top left corner. The keeper got a hand to it but it had too much power on the shot and went in. Oh yeah! I celebrated with the floss and the whole team joined in with the amazing dance move. Even Kiko the goalkeeper flossed like crazy (well, he tried to at least). Our good mood didn't last long when Juventus scored two goals in the second half. That's how the scoreline stayed until injury time when we got another penalty.

Everyone who supported Leeds had their fingers cross that I would score the winning goal. This time, I felt nervous and could really feel the pressure of letting everyone down if I missed. I took three breaths and it felt like everything was in slow motion. I shot at the bottom right corner and the keeper dived the right way, but not in time. The crowd exploded, the noise was deafening! I slid on my knees in celebration but I suddenly felt an awful pain in my knee. I had twisted my knee and damaged my ligaments. I had to be stretchered off the pitch.

I realised I wouldn't kick a ball for six months. That was the best and worst day of my life!

Caden Pickles (8)
Cliffe Primary School, Cliffe

The Incredible Diary Of... Rocket Ralph Supreme

Dear Diary,

For my birthday I got an adorable doll for while my mum was pregnant. At first, the doll was quite annoying but then I got used to it. Every day, I wanted to take him for a walk while no one was looking.

The next day, I went on a different passage. On that path, there were loads of bumps. I couldn't find the wheelchair that I bought so I used one of those garden things to put gardening stuff in. When I went down the path, there was this really big bump that I did not see. When I went over it, the baby fell out!

When I got back home, that was when I realised that the baby was not in the garden thing. I was devastated when I saw that he was gone. But I wanted to get a new baby who was exactly the same but Mum and Dad didn't let me, so I stomped up into my room.

The next day, my mum had to go to the hospital because she was having a baby. When she had the baby, I wasn't that sad anymore. My friends from school were very interested. My friends were called Forren, John and Meia.

The next day, it was Friday, which is show and tell. On Fridays, I always had something to show and tell, even if it was very stupid. That time, I had my new baby brother. My mum and dad had to come over and do the show and tell with me because the baby was very delicate and fragile.

Charlotte Topping (7)
Cliffe Primary School, Cliffe

The Incredible Diary Of... Cinderella

Dear Diary,

Today has been the best day ever! I went to the ball at the king's castle. I saw my two ugly step-sisters there, but luckily, they didn't see me. Once the prince and his dad, the king, saw me, they knew I was the right girl to marry the prince. Then the best thing happened: the prince asked me to dance!

I accidentally stood on his foot, but he just smiled. The prince's smile was beautiful and his voice was like an angel's and, after that dance, we fell in love. But then the clock struck midnight and, at that same moment, the prince proposed to me. I thought of how my life would change and then agreed.

Dear Diary,

Today is the day my life changed because I was going to become a princess! My dear prince forced my stepmother and step-sisters to be our servants. The wedding was great, I wore a beautiful, long, white dress and the prince wore a lovely, black suit. My ring was amazing, it had real diamonds in it too! Now my life is lovely, I have a warm bed, good food and a gentle family.

I don't need this diary anymore, my prince bought me a new one!

Grace Wilson (9)
Cliffe Primary School, Cliffe

The Incredible Diary Of... Harry Parkinson

Dear Diary,

I got a new pet and his name is Toddy. You'll never guess what type of animal he is. He's a frog! He is four years old and his birthday is on the 11th of April and my birthday is on the 11th of April too! The other night, Toddy jumped out of my window and I didn't realise until 9am, but I was busy and couldn't go out and find him until 1pm! I set off to find Toddy, I went to all of his favourite places, but I didn't see any trace of him.

I spent four days trying to find Toddy, but I just couldn't. Last night, I said to myself, "I want to be with Toddy." As soon as the words had passed my lips, I felt a tingle in my toes.

Just then, a flying carpet zoomed out of the sky, it said, "Hop on."

I climbed on the carpet and, as soon as I sat down, it flew off to where I knew the Lake District was. As soon as it turned a corner, I saw a huge castle as black as night and a bright orange door which I thought was pretty silly.

I dropped to the ground, right outside the open door...

Phoebe Weatherall (8)

Cliffe Primary School, Cliffe

82

The Incredible Diary Of... The Incredible James Bond

Dear Diary,

Today I went to Mexico and exploded a building. I went into a helicopter. I was chasing a man down. I kicked a man out of the helicopter. I shot the pilot and flew the helicopter away and crashed it, then I came back to England and went underground and got a new gun (which was a pistol) and there were so many men. One of them had a shotgun so I took him down and stole his shotgun. I jumped across to the next building.

I came to the conclusion that I would get another man's gun, which was a SPAS, and then I got a grenade and blew a building up and must have killed about fifteen men. I found a cave and went into it and it led to a man. He was the man that I had been trying to get to. He was planning his next attack.

So I got my shotgun and I fired and *boom!* He was dead.

That was my diary for today.

Louie Dollimore (8)

Cliffe Primary School, Cliffe

The Incredible Diary Of... The Magic Dolphin

Dear Diary,

This week was crazy! I was playing with Shelly. While I was counting, I opened my eyes just in time to see Shelly struggling in a brown, holey-like thing! She was being swept away from me, past the barriers of the ocean. I was struck by terror, wide-eyed, mouth gaping open, my fins didn't flap one bit!

Suddenly, the entire ocean felt empty and I felt incredibly small. Then I pulled myself together, I was off like a bullet trying to catch up with the terrible thing that took my friend.

After a while of searching, there wasn't a trace of her, nor any other sea creatures! I was very confused and worried. Before long, I met another dolphin, his name was Mason. He was in search of a friend too! Not a turtle, but a seahorse called Nikki. The strange brown thing had swept up his friend too!

He managed to follow it and get a glimpse, it was nothing like he'd ever seen before and made a thunderous, peculiar sound.

Without realising, we had embarked on an adventure to try and find our friends.

Tajana Baxter (9)
Cliffe Primary School, Cliffe

The Incredible Diary Of... The Adventure

Dear Diary,

I saw a bunch of animals today. The animals were two sloths and two dogs. We kept them because all of my friends live with me because we're friends with the animals. But, we had to take them back to the forest because they were a handful. After we put them back, a lion attacked them so we saved them and we took them to another home and then we played a game of dog cards and a game of sloth cards. Then we went for a walk. The dogs ran and the sloths got piggybacks. Then we went back home and went back to the forest and found more animals, two rabbits and two cats and we took them home and had a party! The food was for humans and dogs and sloths and rabbits and cats and we all had a lovely time! We went to bed because it is my birthday tomorrow!

Molly Richardson (8)

Cliffe Primary School, Cliffe

The Incredible Diary Of... The Funniest Day

Dear Diary,

This morning was the funniest I have ever had in my life. So, I shall tell you. It was a school night last night, then, when I got up, I put my school uniform on. After that, I went downstairs and got my breakfast. I sat down on the chair, put my food on the table and started drinking and eating. Then I got back up and, again, got some milk. Then I sat down and got my breakfast. Then my brother came down and pulled the funniest face ever while I was drinking my milk. Then the milk came spraying out of my nose!

Annie Greenwood (9)
Cliffe Primary School, Cliffe

The Incredible Diary Of...

Dear Diary,

My dad loves motocross and has always dreamed of being in it, he was really good and really fast. His first bike was a Yamaha which isn't very fast and it's not even an offroad bike, but you can use it in the mud because all bikes are the same. The reason why he got so good at riding bikes is that he practised and became really good.

Jaydn Williams (9)
Cliffe Primary School, Cliffe

The Incredible Diary Of... The Day I Caused The Earth To Shake

Dear Diary,

Under the Earth's crust I slowly floated around, it was very calm. Suddenly, my enemy nudged my shoulder and bashed me. My anger got really reckless so my knuckles were so tight, I started to tremble. After the enemy came, I pushed back and my shaking caused my anger to go wild.

My ferocious, violent anger was not enough to describe my enemy. I pushed him down as I went up. Meanwhile, I made my anger go but I could not take it so the Earth cracked in half at the top. Buildings started to shake violently.

As my power was destruction and anger, I made weak houses fall like defeated soldiers. They broke into crumbled bits of rock and stone. After the deadly, aggressive shaking stopped I saw the destruction that I had caused. I felt very ashamed of myself. What did I do?

I feel guilty now. I wish anger was not a thing. I should feel guilty people were killed. It's only me and Earth now.

Saffron Rose Stamper (8)

Green Gates Primary School, Redcar

The Incredible Diary Of... The Day I Erupted

Dear Diary,

Early this morning, was a day of dangerous disaster! I was bubbling viciously deep under the Earth's solid crust and I flowed toxically like thick treacle. As my crimson, molten, orange liquid burned dangerously, I journeyed far under the surface, towards the conduit, grumbling like the stomach of a dragon. I was transforming from magma...

While the tension rose, I loudly trickled through the infinite tunnel and burst into the vent like a flaming firework. Pressure started to build and I pushed my way up to the giant mouth of the volcano. Preparing to explode. Out of control, my sticky, smoking liquid erupted in a burst of blinding, bright light. Dancing flames, gloriously soaring into the clear air above. *Bang!*

Into the immense blue sky above, I separated into ash and lava, creating a huge, deadly cloud of ash. As the suffocating, dark grey cloud grew larger and larger, all to be seen was pure darkness from the darkest shadow of ash. Meanwhile, my boiling liquid flowed rapidly like treacle. Down the rocky mountainside, destroying everything in my path. Devastation!

As quick as a flash, I threateningly travelled towards the turquoise, green grass at the base of the grey mountain. I set alight nature's delightful riches until flickering flames danced in a blur of molten and crimson.

Journeying forward in vicious aggression I excitedly found my destination. With a roar like a dangerous tiger, I zoomed towards the poor buildings, making them crumble to the ground's concrete before burying them below my burning body.

Stampeding through the rocky, bumpy streets of Pompeii, I destroyed everything in my way. Nothing was left standing alive. The streets of Pompeii were totally buried under my smoky, hot liquid.

As all the buildings crumbled to the ground, I let off giant flames. As I journeyed through Pompeii and furiously took down more and more buildings, I felt as hot as a dragon's fire! I rushed down the roads as fast as lightning. As I zoomed down the roads, giant buildings collapsed. I heard screams all over Pompeii. I had started to cool and relax but I couldn't hear anything. I destroyed all of Pompeii.

Now I have destroyed Pompeii. I feel ashamed, depressed and sad.

Ethan Brooklyn Mazfari (8)
Green Gates Primary School, Redcar

The Incredible Diary Of... The Day I Erupted

An extract

Dear Diary,

Earlier this morning, was a day of total devastation! I was bubbling violently deep under the Earth's surface and I flowed rapidly like thick treacle. As my crimson and orange, molten liquid burned furiously, I travelled far under the surface, towards the conduit, grumbling like a furious lion ready for dinner. I was transforming from magma...

While the tension rose, I smoothly trickled through the never-ending tunnel and burst into the vent like an exploding firework. Pressure started to build and I pushed my way up to the gigantic mouth of the volcano, preparing to explode. Out of control, my scorching, smoking liquid erupted in a burst of blinding light and dancing flames, gloriously soaring into the clear air above. *Whoosh!*

Soaring into the bright cerulean sky above, grey ash separated from the volcano which caused suffocation. Ash was hurting all living things, suffocating animals and growing into a vast cloud of darkness above. Meanwhile, my scorching, molten liquid flowed rapidly down the steep mountain like treacle. Unstoppable.

As quick as a flash, I dangerously travelled towards the bright, green grass at the base of the steamy mountain seeking out my deadly prey. In a moment of fury, I set alight nature's life until dancing flames danced in the colour of yellow and red.

Crashing forward in furious anger I happily found my destination. With a hiss like a hunting snake, I zoomed towards silent buildings, making them crumble to the ground before burying them below my boiling liquid.

Rapidly stampeding into the silent town, destroying buildings all around me in my path. Everything was completely buried underneath my molten, crimson liquid. All buildings and life were nowhere to be seen. Burying people and buildings by my scorching, hot liquid...

Riley Watson (8)
Green Gates Primary School, Redcar

The Incredible Diary Of… The Day I Erupted

24th August, 79AD

Dear Diary,

As quick as a flash I blew into the cerulean sky and I separated into puffs and lava which created a deadly grey cloud of ash, which choked the land. The vast ash cloud grew bigger and bigger until it was the only light for all living things. Meanwhile, my blinking, fiery liquid flew down the slopes of the rocky mountain like a river blown by wind. Devastation! As quick as a flash, I viciously travelled towards the bright, green grass at the base of the rocky volcano, seeking out my prey. In a moment of viciousness, I set alight nature's property until blinking fire made a sight of blurriness.

Running towards in extreme fury, I excitably found my destination. With a groan like a beast's stomach, I leapt towards unsuspecting buildings, making them crumble to the ground before burying them below my blazing body.

Rushing through Pompeii, I swallowed every bit of Pompeii. I made the buildings rumble and tumble to the ground. My crimson, blazing body followed behind and fetched all the silent buildings I didn't get.

I ran through the bustling town of Pompeii and killed all life.

I buried the bustling town of Pompeii with my blinking, boiling body. Not even a rooftop was to be seen when I covered Pompeii.

After, I started to slow down and my anger started to calm. When my anger was properly calm, I stopped and turned from a burning machine to a silent rock! I was no danger to anything so my job here was done. I was a bold, black rock for the rest of my life. This is my only life. As I cooled I was steaming but the steam started to go. I was stuck in the same spot and was not touched for a long time.

I am now a rock that has been through a story. Today was the day of mass destruction because of me. I feel guilty and ashamed of myself.

Alfie Harrison (8)

Green Gates Primary School, Redcar

The Incredible Diary Of... The Day I Erupted

Dear Diary,

Today was a day of destruction! I was bubbling violently deep underground and I flowed like thick treacle. My crimson, molten liquid burned viciously under the Earth's surface, towards the conduit which was grumbling like the roar of a lion. I was transforming from magma...

While the tension rose, I slowly trickled through the never-ending tunnel and burst into the vent like a bomb. Pressure started to build and I pushed my way up to the huge mouth of a volcano, preparing to burst out of control, my sticky, smoking liquid erupted in a burst of blinding light and dancing flames, gloriously soaring into the clear air above. *Whoosh!*

High above, in the never-ending sky, I had split into lava and grey ash cloud and made a giant ash cloud, suffocating the clear air above. The expanse of grey grew bigger and bigger until it took over the entire sky, casting a depressing shadow over the land below. Meanwhile, my scorching liquid flowed down the slopes of a dangerous mountain, rapidly like a rushing waterfall. Unstoppable!

As quick as a flash, I rapidly travelled towards the luscious green grass at the base of the smoky slopes until flickering flames in a blur of crimson red and yellow.

Rushing forwards in violent anger I excitedly found my destination. With the roar of a bear, I surged towards incoherent buildings, making them crumble to the ground before burying them below my scorching body.

Stampeding through stone buildings of Pompeii, I reached the houses in my path. No life was left untouched by my lethality, no animals were alive, everything was destroyed. Everyone dying. I was taking over Pompeii.

I was slowing down, turning into black rock.

A silent town. Everything buried underground. I was still. I felt guilty, ashamed and desolate.

Kaiden Craig Taylor (8)

Green Gates Primary School, Redcar

The Incredible Diary Of... The Day I Erupted

Dear Diary,

Early this morning, total disaster struck! Rapidly bubbling like a witch's cauldron deep under the Earth's crust, I started to dangerously rumble. My flaming, sticky, molten liquid exploded into an ocean of devastation. Rapid waves as hot as the sun viciously swirled towards the conduit. I was transforming from magma...

While I rose, I quickly travelled through the never-ending tunnel and burst into the vent like a flaming firework. I started to build up to the runny mouth of the volcano, preparing to pounce out. Out of control, my sticky, smoky liquid erupted in a burst of blinding light and dancing flames, gloriously soaring into the air around. *Whoosh!* Into the deep cerulean sky, I separated into ash and lava, creating an immense ash cloud. The ash and lava covered the land with a deadly shadow. My molten lava was flowing down the sides of the rocky mountain. Deadly. As quick as a flash, I threateningly travelled towards the green grass at the base, seeking out my prey. In a moment of devastation, I set alight Nature until dancing flames lit with a splash of yellow and orange.

Pouncing forwards in anger, I happily found my destination. With a growl like a rumbling belly, I travelled towards scorching buildings making the ground rumble before burying their fiery bodies and running into the streets of Pompeii which I wrecked and destroyed! Everything was gone. When I began to slow and cool the orange liquid turned to black and my fire went out and turned to smoke. I transformed f a terrifying monster into still and silent volcanic rock. I meant no harm. Today was a day of total destruction because of me. I am exhausted and ashamed.

Harriet Brocklesby-Brown (7)

Green Gates Primary School, Redcar

The Incredible Diary Of... The Day I Caused The Earth To Shake

An extract

Dear Diary,

Today was a total disaster! I was moving quite slow under the Earth's crust until my other friend hit me like a bumper car and the Earth started to shake and tremble. I got so angry that I jumped on him and pushed him down under the Earth's crust. The shaking was horrible. He then became my prisoner.

Buildings started to fall. It was like they were wounded soldiers that went to hurt and fight. The Earth was going down because of me and because of what I had done. I was getting angrier and I was letting out more and more energy when the Earth shook and gave a very loud shake! Pretty buildings were defeated and were crushed by me. Houses were gone, no life was left. All of the living things had been vanished and never seen again. Then I got so angry, the Earth started to crack and it had split into two pieces. It was like I strangled the Earth with my power!

I started to slow down, I was calm. I was surrounded with bits of crumbled, dusty buildings and houses. All this mess, what did I do? It was terrible! I felt that I made all this mess and terror for nothing. All that was left was silence. Somehow I managed to keep half the buildings up but other than that there was nothing left! People had been shaken so hard that they were killed. I stopped and slowed down even more. What I did was terrible! I sat in silence. I wanted to start over again and if I crashed I would be more gentle than I was. I now feel guilty and ashamed!

Faye George (8)
Green Gates Primary School, Redcar

The Incredible Diary Of... The Day I Caused The Earth To Shake

Dear Diary,

Today was the day of devastation! I was slowly moving under the expansive Earth's crust as I felt a nudge on my shoulder. My anger rose up and I began to get angrier as I moved to continents. I rose more and more and the Earth had a small tremble and shook a bit aggressively. It was not a calm and still Earth after he bumped into me. Why would he be so careless?

I was so angry. I pushed on top of him so he was underneath me. The Earth was split into two parts from my temper. It was violent and devastating and the Earth was shaking more and more. Meanwhile, the crack in the Earth was massive and more violent. Buildings started to shake like a leaf in the wind. Weary! High-pitch screaming was everywhere and babies were crying everywhere. I crashed. People were running out of buildings screaming and crying. Weak, flimsy buildings shook.

Crash! went the buildings as they fell. They fell like wounded soldiers on a battlefield. There was a lot of devastation! Everything was gone, nothing was left untouched in my path. Still and silent it was. Deadly!

My anger is gone, everything is gone. I feel guilty and ashamed for what I did today on the Earth. I feel sorry for many people I killed.

Grace Proud (8)
Green Gates Primary School, Redcar

The Incredible Diary Of... The Day I Caused The Earth To Shake

Dear Diary,

Today was a day of disaster! I was calmly moving deep underground of the circular Earth. All of a sudden, I felt a brush against me and it was another tectonic plate and we caused a very dangerous tremble in the green and blue Earth. It was a level one (the rating goes up to twelve and it was a level one). *Really, a level one? I wanted it to be a level two!*

Anger built and I aggressively pushed back the other tectonic plate. I carefully went over the top, pushing my enemy down. It was violent and aggressive. The Earth shook more violently until my anger couldn't be contained! I split the Earth into two and made a horrible crack in the Earth's surface. It was like a fight in school but it was on the Earth, not at school.

All of the buildings started to shake like leaves in the wind. Panic was all around us. Buildings began to fall like wounded soldiers and towns became pits of rubble and stone. It began to turn into total destruction. Cities were flattened. Still and silent. Tremors stopped.

Nothing is left. I feel guilty and ashamed of myself. Anger is all gone... My energy was all filled up and now it's gone!

Calvin Lewis McMahon (8)

Green Gates Primary School, Redcar

The Incredible Diary Of... The Day I Erupted

An extract

Dear Diary,

Early this morning total disaster struck! Rapidly bubbling like a witch's cauldron deep under the Earth's crust, I started to rumble. My flaming, sticky liquid exploded in an ocean of devastation as rapid waves as hot as the sun swirled towards conflict. I transformed from magma...

While the tension rose, I quietly trickled through the deep, dark tunnels and burst into the vent. Pressure started to build and I pushed my way up through the mouth of the volcano, preparing to explode in fiery flames. Smoke filled the sky and ash clouds grew into the clear sky above. I split into ash and lava, making an ash cloud of dark grey, suffocating life all around. The ash grew bigger and bigger until darkness converted the entire sky. Meanwhile, my liquid flowed like an ocean of devastation down the huge mountain. Quickly I spread around, forming rock and destruction around the world.

Daisie Bennett (8)

Green Gates Primary School, Redcar

106

The Incredible Diary Of... The Day I Caused The Earth To Shake

Dear Diary,

Today was the day of devastation! It happened when I was calmly moving innocently and peacefully but then I felt a hard nudge on my body. My tectonic plate filled with rage and anger, then I started to push back horrifically! All of a sudden there was an earthquake.

Then the Earth's crust started to shake, also the buildings did too. The earthquake's strong power got so violent, residents' houses got destroyed and tumbled like a game of Jenga. A crack split the Earth in two in the centre. Meanwhile, the building kept on falling to dust.

People desperately rushed to safety so they didn't get caught in the terrifying earthquake but some people couldn't get to safety. They couldn't escape as the furious earthquake trapped them. All of the city was destroyed. Buildings fell onto people. Total destruction. Silence! I feel ashamed and disappointed.

Amelia Wilcock (7)

Green Gates Primary School, Redcar

The Incredible Diary Of... The Day I Caused The Earth To Shake

Dear Diary,
The Earth began to shake because of my tectonic plates. When I crashed together, I made an earthquake. When my two parts crashed together, an earthquake began to shoot roughly.
No living things survived this mega-destructive earthquake. I split the Earth's surface and everyone fell below the crust. They were buried and fell like wounded soldiers and became my prisoners.
The buildings were too weak against the earthquake. Windows and foundations were broken because of the violent earthquake. Everything was broken in this world. This world was completely destroyed.
I feel guilty and ashamed that I did this. I broke people's homes and now they are homeless. I split the Earth in two and the people fell into the crack in the middle of the blazing Earth.

Keagan Lee Addison (7)
Green Gates Primary School, Redcar

The Incredible Diary Of... The Day I Erupted

Dear Diary,

Today was the day of disaster! I was bubbling dangerously deep under the Earth's surface and I flowed smoothly like treacle. As my crimson and orange blinding liquid burned furiously, I travelled far under the surface, towards the conduit, grumbling like the belly of a beast. I was transforming from magma.

While the tension rose, I calmly trickled through the never-ending tunnel and burst into the vent like a shooting star. Pressure started to build and I pushed my way up to the wide mouth of the volcano. Preparing to explode out of control, my sticky liquid erupted in a burst of blinding light and dancing flames, gloriously soaring into the air above. *Whoosh!*

Kenzie Deej Mcpake (8)

Green Gates Primary School, Redcar

The Incredible Diary Of... Me And Ronaldo

Dear Diary,

I want to tell you about what's happened in my life... I went to Italy to join Juventus. I met Ronaldo. I was called Ronaldo Jr but it didn't end there. Barcelona bought me then I saw Messi then PSG bought me. I saw Mbappé and Neymar, then Manchester United bought me then I met Pogba, Young and David de Gea.

I felt so happy but I wanted to play for Juventus. We lost but Juventus bought me again. We played - Juventus vs PSG. It was a good match. It was 5-3 to Juventus. I scored four of the goals and Ronaldo scored one goal. For PSG Mbappé scored two goals and Neymar scored one goal. Ronaldo was crying because there was a person called Ronaldo Jr. And, because there had never been a Ronaldo Jr before, he gave me his golden Ferrari, Lamborghini, Porsche and minibus!

Cayden Mayes (9)

Kestrel Class - Danesgate, York

The Incredible Diary Of... The Sword

Dear Diary,

A boy saw me in a rock. He tried to get me but I couldn't get out so he went back home. He went on the computer to make a machine to get me out of the rock and it worked. I was delighted. I went back home and then some bad guys appeared. We fought so much and then, victory! We won!

After two hours of fighting, we relaxed for the rest of the day.

Charlie Kilner-Marshall (9)

Kestrel Class - Danesgate, York

The Incredible Diary Of... Kevin The Cat

Dear Diary,

Before I start, I am happy to announce that this is my first diary entry and hopefully not the last.

I was once being cuddled by my owner and she was daydreaming.

She said to me, "If you ever write a diary (which you won't, you're a cat) then make sure you include my details in case you lose it and a cute boy finds it." So here they are: Her name is Bella and she likes cats. I won't include her number partly because I don't know it and partly because a creepy person could find it and that's not good. So I'm making part of her daydreams come true. Anyway, the real reason I started today is that I've had a particularly exciting day. Today was the first day I was allowed to go outside with my brother, Smudge. Bella and her sister were bouncing on the trampoline and Smudge was on the garden wall. I wanted to do something exciting. The garden wall? No, too low. The house roof? Too high. Then I saw it. *Bingo,* I thought. It was a tree! I'm a cat and cats climb trees! It was a brilliant idea!

I went over the wall and leapt onto a branch. This was so exciting! Even better than harassing Bella in the night. As I was slowly getting higher, I heard a strange cat talking to me.

"Get down here, you silly thing!" It said. "You'll get stuck if you don't."

I looked down and saw a girl cat.

"I'll be fine!" I said.

I climbed higher and higher until I reached the top. *Time to get down,* I thought. I looked down. It was so high, like the Eiffel Tower, maybe even higher!

"Help!" I yelled.

"What did I tell you? I knew you'd get stuck," said the female cat, "give me one second." And like that, she was gone.

A couple of minutes later, Bella and her sister came and shouted, "Come down Kevin!"

How do you expect me to come down when I'm stuck on an Eiffel Tower tree? I thought.

Soon my other owner, who Bella calls mum, came with a very tall man with a ladder. Before I knew it, Mum was climbing up the ladder to get me. She grabbed me and took me into the house, where I mostly ate and drank milk.

So I think we've all learnt a valuable lesson here. Never ever, ever climb Eiffel Tower trees unless you're a trained professional.
Well, goodbye for now,
Kevin the cat.

Isabella Freeman (11)
Nawton Community Primary School, Nawton

The Incredible Diary Of... Alfie

Dear Diary,

Today me, Harrison and Oscar went to Liverpool to see them play, it was really fun and exciting but after the match, there was a fight...

7pm

In the fight we were all in the middle, it was really loud! All different emotions came through our heads. We were sweating, scared and emotional. We did not know what to do, there was a load of scary people swarming around us, all of the people were City fans. We didn't have any idea what to say when a scary man came to us and said, "Why do you have a Liverpool top on?"

We said, "We don't know..."

"Why, I asked you," he said.

"Oh, it's because my auntie made us!" I said.

"Okay," he said.

9pm

Still, all of the people were searching around us then I had an idea... It was risky but good. We had to go through their legs.

"Let's go! Yay, we did it!" we said.

Alfie Blacklock (10)

Nawton Community Primary School, Nawton

The Incredible Diary Of... Jake Helen

Dear Diary,

At 7:55pm, I woke up. I jumped out of my bed and got dressed then rushed downstairs, had my breakfast and went out. I bolted to my dad's police station and sprinted through the doors. I ran to my dad and said, "Sorry, I am late."

"No problem," he said, "could you go and get me a coffee?"

"Yep!" I panted then ran to the coffee machine.

I quickly got the drink and slowly walked to his office and opened the door and gave it to him.

"Do you need anything else?"

"No thank you."

"Okay, I'll go on my computer then!" I exclaimed, then ran to my space and started.

A couple of hours later, I got called to my dad's office so I could help with a little case. When I finally got to his office, he said, "Could you do some research on the National Bank?"

"Okay," I sighed.

Halfway into my research, I found out the amount of money and that it had been stolen and found a description of the man, his car and where he could have fled to.

"This is great!" I bellowed then raced to my dad's office. "Dad, Dad, I've found some info about it! It's been broken into!"

"I know that, tell me something I don't know!"

"But I've got a description of the man, his car and where he could have fled to."

"Brill, could you direct us to where he is?"

"Sure!" I told him to go to Highcross Road.

When we arrived, there was a plethora of police cars already there. When they told me to go in with my dad. I was scared but ecstatic, as I walked in the door creaked. We strolled around, slowly downstairs then we went upstairs and what we found was horrible.

We found an immense amount of money in one of the rooms but in another, we found a man in the corner of the room that matched the description.

"Sir, please stand up and follow me."

"Okay!"

After that, we got all the money and the guy was arrested. My dad was pleased with me for finding and giving back half a million pounds to the bank. So he kindly upped my allowance because I'd sought out a criminal, so it ended up good.

Archie Welford (10)

Nawton Community Primary School, Nawton

The Incredible Diary Of... Sam And The Volcano

Dear Diary,

I cannot believe what happened today. As the sun rose, I turned and moved in bed, not being able to sleep. I slumped out of bed, suddenly forgetting where I was. *I am on holiday*, I told myself. At breakfast, at a nearby cafe, I was eating, when I heard a rumbling sound. Confused, startled and anxious, I dashed out the room to see what the commotion was.

I tore through the streets, ignoring everyone and pushing past people. I finally reached my apartment and rushed to my room. I grabbed my stuff and left for the volcano. Within sight of the volcano, I darted forward. My heart missed a beat. My heart pounded. What should I do? I sprinted forward, leaping over stones and rocks. I charged on. The rumbling just got louder. As I drew nearer, I spotted an opening in the rock. Someone was walking out of the jagged rock. I crept forward silently.

"I flicked the switch, the volcano will erupt," said the first man.

"Great!" replied the second man.

I knew I had to do something.

As soon as they left, I knew time was running out, so I sprinted forwards. With my heart pounding, I entered the deep, dark and damp maze. I grabbed my torch and ran further into the maze. I did not have long. It was cold in the maze so I kept moving. Suddenly I stopped... In my way was a pit of bones and skeletons. I considered what I would do. I made up my mind. I waded through.

After, I started running again. Not long after, I came to another challenge. This time sinking sand. *Now this will be tough*, I thought. There was a thin bar at the side of the sinking sand.

I jumped on the bar, holding onto the wall. *How much longer?* I thought to myself...

Harrison Bryant (10)
Nawton Community Primary School, Nawton

The Incredible Diary Of... Jake Mathew

Dear Diary,

I want to tell you about my day... I heard something downstairs like a window breaking. The teachers were still asleep. I leaned against the wall to Emma's dorm to see if she was awake. I heard her breathing.

I whispered, "Emma, are you okay?"

She whispered back, "Yes!"

I crept down the ladder of the bunk bed.

00:00

I opened the door. It creaked so loudly it made my ears ring, but nobody woke up! I knocked on Emma's door. She answered, panting like a dog.

"Calm down!" I said.

"Breathe slowly!"

She took a deep breath. The rumours were true, I guess, it is a haunted residential.

I whispered, "I'm going to see what happened."

"Be careful," she murmured.

I ran downstairs where I heard the noise in the lounge room. The key from the door was bent. I tried to unbend it but it wouldn't budge. Emma came downstairs.

She told me, "I bet it was a worker tidying up and he made one loud bang."

I asked her, "How do you explain the key then?"

Emma said, "It's probably always been like that. Come on, I'll prove it to you."

1:00am

She opened the door and in one shot she was on the floor bleeding! As soon as he had fired the gun, I called the police. They were there in an instant and arrested him.

A day later, Emma is okay and well. The police gave me a medal and I got a special mention in class. I went to see Emma in hospital and she was indeed okay and healthy.

Wow! That was a roller coaster of a week!

Scarlett Bo Savic (10)
Nawton Community Primary School, Nawton

The Incredible Diary Of... The Wondrous Whirlpool Adventure

Dear Diary,

You may already know this but here's a quick reminder (as I haven't written in here for years). Hi, I'm Millie, I grew up in Texas but that was all cities and you guessed it... more cities. That's one reason why I moved here to the Maldives. But the other reason is I have a dream I will travel the world for. I will do anything for. And that dream is to scuba-dive, why? you ask. When I was two, my mother and father took me to the Sea Life Centre. The first step I took I immediately fell in love with all those creatures but one day something awful happened... My father died. He was a scuba diver too so when he died I knew I had to finish the quest and that is what I did.

Splash! I'm in, here we go... Suddenly I came to a halt, I saw a massive whirlpool of sea creatures, it was fascinating, it was like a huge tornado under the sea but something wasn't right about the creatures, they looked alarmed and scared. I suddenly had an urge to save them... Suddenly one hour of waiting slowly passed by and as it did, the fish became more and more alarmed.

Suddenly I was drawn to a shadow. A shadow that had had a figure of a squid but the size of an elephant. Without warning, I had a faint idea of what it was... An octopus suddenly everything slipped into place...

I had to find a way to calm down an octopus, that's impossible right...? Wrong! I had to find a way. I would make everything right again. I would make a puppet octopus (Penelope) and the alarmed octopus (Gregory) will fall for her charm. Right, let's go...

Megan Ryder (11)
Nawton Community Primary School, Nawton

The Incredible Diary Of... Jess Blacklock

Dear Diary,

Today was amazing, today I got B+ in maths, today at my private school. I told Mr Lost about my bullying. It was fabulous.

First, this morning, when I woke up, I got dressed, strolled downstairs, grabbed my breakfast bar (that Mum left out last night) then I picked up my old red school bag, slipped on my battered shoes and walked out the door. I felt so happy.

Unfortunately, when I got to school, the bullies were there, they started singing a song. I hate them... 'She's got a long nose, big ears, little mouth, she smells with a battered red bag, she's a failure...'

But then I decided that I'd had enough. I'm going to go big guns (Mr Lost, our headteacher).

Thirty minutes later, Mr Lost came to the rescue. He told them off and gave all nine of them a detention. The bell rang so I trotted along to class. First class, always the worst. Then the day really started. At 9:45 the class began. But today was test day. Test day, it sounds the worst but it's not too bad. It's just a day with a maths test, an English test, a science test and the worst - a music test.

"Jess Blacklock!" our maths teacher shouted at the end of the test. "Come here now!"

I was scared but I did and he said, "Well done, you got a B+!"

I was so proud. When I got home, I told Mum about my day. And then I wrote in my diary and I'm just about to stop. This was my day and I hope you enjoyed reading about it.

Jess Blacklock (11)

Nawton Community Primary School, Nawton

The Incredible Diary Of... Chip

Dear Diary,

Yesterday I left my family, sad I know. Even though I left to live with the wonderful Kendalls, I still miss my real family. I might never see them again so I love them to the moon and back. When I left my sisters, Echo and Ruby, they gave me the biggest lick ever and my old owners, Tim and Sheila, hugged me so much.

Here is something I have never told you, Diary, before... My full name is Chipotle Pepper, I was born on the 20th June, 2018 and the vets thought I was a girl, crazy I know! But my old owners found out I was a boy when Tim was de-fleaing me.

Right, back to today... So when they came to pick me up, I thought it was the vet, every dog's worst nightmare, but they were my new owners. When they saw me, I could tell their hearts rose with joy! The parents clapped their hands together and the kids jumped out of their socks. My tail wagged so much it nearly fell off! They stayed for a bit and were told what I ate and how much. Then they picked me up, put me in the back with Louie and Neve and set off.

When we got to their house, there was a nanny, a grandad and a friend in her teens. I was shown to my bed, it was luxurious. The bed was blue and there was a crate and a toy pheasant called Picky. They adore me. When my spotlight of fame was over, I curled up and slept for five minutes then woke up and my energy levels were 100%. I was ready to play again until my energy level was 50%. It was nine o'clock before I got to sleep again.

Neve Kendall (10)

Nawton Community Primary School, Nawton

The Incredible Diary Of... The First World Cup And Best

Dear Diary,

I am here again, yes it's me, Jack. Today was the best day of my life! England, the team I played for, got through the finals against Brazil. I knew it would be a hard game and I was in the starting eleven. I am only eighteen years old. We were in the changing rooms. We got changed to play the match. There were about six million people at the match. We all had a laugh before the match. My mum and dad rang me up saying good luck and they played the National Anthem. This was my dream when I was just ten.

I said to myself, "I want to play in the World Cup Finals." There it was... the World Cup.

The whistle blew. We took the kick-off. Three minutes in, I was in the box, it crossed to me and I shot and... goal! We were winning 1-0. Neymar shot and scored. 1-1. I was running and got fouled and took the freekick. I shot. It curled and top bins and scored 2-1. Half-time. They took kick-off and missed. Neymar scored 2-2. Harry Kane shot and missed. Neymar shot and missed. It went to extra time. First half no one scored, last half I overhead kicked and... goal! 3-2.

We'd won the World Cup, *yessss!* All of the Brazil fans and team were crying but England's fans and team were happy. I went up to the referee and collected the match ball. The all England team were getting ready for me. I went up to the podium and lifted the World Cup and I went back to the changing rooms.

Jack Everett (10)
Nawton Community Primary School, Nawton

The Incredible Diary Of... Sky The Rescue Dog

Dear Diary,

Today was finally the day I got to do what I have been training for, but first let me explain myself. My name is Sky and I have been a rescue dog for over two years. I am a Labrador and the day had come. I just took a four-hour flight to get to Mexico. They made me take a white pill but it was covered in peanut butter so that was okay. I am slightly nervous but I am with my owner and I trust him as I have been with him all my life. When I finally got to the scene, it was horrible. I knew from my training that it was an earthquake. I felt a gentle hand on my back. I knew it was him and all my nerves vanished. Time to put those weird boots on that make my paws warm. It was time for action. I smelt a lady who was still young and had definitely been eating sausages - I know that for a fact.

Suddenly the Earth began to rumble and shake. The earthquake was still ongoing. In a panic, I scrambled away to find others stuck further away. I was in such a rush I didn't realise that the earthquake had stopped.

By that time, I was well away from my owner. I knew he would find me and I had a vague smell of the way I came so I wasn't so worried. Then, just as I was on a trail for an old man, something else started to mix in with the scent, it was the smell of crime and evil - it wasn't good. My curiosity grew until I knew that I had to find out what it was...

India Steele (11)

Nawton Community Primary School, Nawton

The Incredible Diary Of... Scout And The Haunted House

Friday 23rd December, 2018

Dear Diary,

Today was the worst day ever. I moved to this awful new house. It's haunted, there are cobwebs everywhere, spiders, and I can even hear noises when I go to sleep. It's so creepy. Here's the story so far...

11:00

It all started at the kennels, when someone said, "I like this dog, what's it called?"

"Scout," said the man.

"Okay, I'll buy this one."

So off I went, wagging my tail and leaving the kennels behind me and moving into a new house. When I got there, the house had flowers on the outside and even had a play area for me. The lady got out of the car and opened the house door. It was massive.

12:00

"Lunchtime!" the lady called.

On the table, there was chicken, lamb, beef and fish, every dog's dream. I even had my own chair. It took me four hours to eat my lunch. I was so tired I fell asleep. When I woke up, it was 21:00. I could hear noises. I thought it was the lady but she was asleep. I went down the stairs but there was nothing there. Then something fell off the shelf... It was a tin of beans. I could hear footprints coming towards me. I thought it was the lady again but the footprints were too big for her size. Then I could hear a noise like 'ha ha ha' and 'ooooo'. It scared the life out of me...

Annie Foster (10)

Nawton Community Primary School, Nawton

The Incredible Diary Of... The Tortoise Plan

Dear Diary,

I was so excited. Finally my big day! I had worked it all out. I could just imagine on BBT Radio Tortoise... The first tortoise to discover the edge of the side. I was speechless. Maybe next I could be the first tortoise on the moon! Or to Mars! What about Saturn? Anyway...

The day passed by. Minutes were hours and hours were hmmm... two hours! I took a nap. I was tossing and turning. I could not get one minute of naptime. I was waiting and waiting. How much longer? It's not fair, the day I went to the vet's, the day flew by. Let's have a look...

Nobody was there so I gave it a go. I was only going to open my cage, climb out and get back in before anybody saw me or else my plan would fail. I sang as I stealthily opened my cage and climbed out... but somebody came. I ran back into my cage. I felt like I'd climbed Mount Everest. I took a nap. A nice nap. I woke up and knew it was time...

Everybody was upstairs, it was 8:30pm. If one thing went wrong, my whole plan would have gone upside down. I followed my plan to get out of the cage. *Thud!*

"Right, let's see what's at the end of the breakfast bar..."

Running faster and faster, closer and closer, I fell...

That night, I dreamt of being the first tortoise on the moon. That was the best day of my whole life!

Jessica Hyde (10)

Nawton Community Primary School, Nawton

The Incredible Diary Of... The Demon Packed House

Dear Diary,

As I pulled up outside the house, a shiver was sent down my spine. I have dealt with houses full of demons before, but not like this one, no, no, no, this one was different. I found the key in the letterbox, I took it out and unlocked the door, a plethora of toxic spirits and demons flushed into me. It was thundering and chucking it down with rain. I was told a demon lingers in the attic so in an instant, I rushed upstairs, strangely to find the attic door already open. I put my ladder up and laid out my Ouija board, I put my two fingers on the plectrum, it went to the 'yes'. My heart was racing now, it said 'Z-O-Z-O', it was Zozo, the evil demon. I stupidly let go and explored the abandoned home...

The cellar had been blocked off years ago, more than a century ago, then the cupboard door flung open. I fled in terror, back to the attic to strangely find my Ouija board had gone.

I strolled anxiously back into the kitchen then I looked at the time, it was 3am, the Devil's Hour. I felt a strange floorboard, I ripped up the carpet to find a trapdoor, the ancient cellar had been found.

I stepped foot in the cellar, I fell backwards and started shouting, "Zozo, Zozo, Zozo!"
I suddenly snapped out and ran and ran out of the home. I got in my car and sped off as fast as I could.

Ross Fahey (10)

Nawton Community Primary School, Nawton

The Incredible Diary Of... Tom And The Room 101

Dear Diary,

10am

Today was the most unusual day of my life. First, me and Jessie were on our way to school, making sure we were not late. We heaved our bags up the hill. We could hear our teacher in the distance, shouting the register. Just then, I heard Mr Cooves call my name. We rushed up the hill. Finally, we got to the top, jumped on the bus and set off to Whitby.

12pm

Bang! We crashed! I was terrified.

I was shouting, "Jessie, Jessie, where are you?"

There was no reply. I searched the bus high and low. Then I saw her... lying dead under the seat of the coach. I thought, *how on Earth am I going to make the residential without her?*

2pm

I stumbled out of the coach, carrying my sterile bag in my dry, dirty hands. I tiptoed up the creaky stairs, carrying Jessie in my arms. She may be dead but I wasn't leaving her.

11pm

I was just turning my light off when I heard footsteps going to Room 101. I stepped out of my room and guess what I saw... More than thirty ghosts. They were all heading to now what was Room 101. Obviously I followed them. I heard music in the distance. I stepped into Room 101 and there stood Jessie. I waved and she waved back.

Evie Dunsmore (10)

Nawton Community Primary School, Nawton

The Day Gizzy Gets His Forever Home

Dear Diary,

Today was a good day, an exciting day and the best day ever! Here's the story so far... I went to the RSPCA Centre to get a dog and I saw the most beautiful dog in the world. Well, in my eyes he was! He was called Gizzy (Gizmo) so I took him home, and when I got home, I started to play with him. Then I found out he was dead shy which made feel really scared and sad but anyway, I still kept on playing with him but just then, there was a knock at the door. It was Annie with her dog, Scout, and Eloise and her dog, Cherry, and Grace with her dog, Tilly.

They all said, "Do you want to come for a walk with us?"

"Yeah, sure thing! Where do you want to go?"

"We do not mind where we go?"

"Oh okay, we can go down to Grace's farm. That will be a nice long walk for them."

So off we went over the soggy field, getting very wet with the dogs. Tilly, Scout, Gizzy and Cherry were loving it but on the other hand, Annie and Grace, Eloise and I were not liking it at all but anyway, we carried on.

When we got to Grace's house, we had to bath the dogs because they were very wet and muddy and that was the best day ever!

Faith Trinity Thatcher (9)

Nawton Community Primary School, Nawton

The Incredible Diary Of... Tilly And The Mystery Friends

Dear Diary,

I cannot believe what happened today... Here's the story...

I moved into a new house and it seemed to be all normal until around lunchtime, when lightbulbs blew and gusts of wind flew through. With woofs of horror and nerves, other strange dogs from the past came galloping down the old, creaky stairs. I jumped back into a corner until I couldn't go any further. I was petrified until a small black and white terrier named Fidget came up to me. She seemed gentle and kind so I told her everything. Hours passed and I still had questions. I asked her why the house was called 'The Dog Hotel'.

She said, "Many years ago, there were two girls called Annie and Grace who set up a charity to look after unwanted and lonely dogs. Their friend, Faith, also helped but they left because something mysterious happened and they left all the dogs... There could only be one answer... Ghosts!

Grace Smith (9)
Nawton Community Primary School, Nawton

The Incredible Diary Of... The Easter Bunny

Dear Diary,

This morning, we were having scrambled egg because it was Easter and the Easter Bunny was coming - but I did not see any eggs! Usually, he hides them really badly because we have a big garden and he forgets where he puts them. That's what I thought - he might have forgotten them or overslept. I decided to look around the house.

When I looked around the house, there were no Easter eggs! I called my BFF, Hanna. I asked my BFF Hanna if she had any eggs. She said no, then she came over.

I heard a knock on the door. I said, "Hanna? Hanna?"

But it was not Hannah - it was a person in a black hoodie with a basket with eggs, but they were hard and they weren't chocolate! I was sad. I called my mother.

I said, "Don't buy any eggs."

I felt sad and so did Hanna - then we heard a noise upstairs. I went to see what it was... then I saw the Easter Bunny! I was as quiet as I could be, then I shouted, "Hanna!"

Kayah Scarlett Matuszewska (8)
St Benedict's RC Primary School, Ampleforth

The Incredible Diary Of... Ellie And The Epic Gang

Dear Diary,

Today, I did something I have never done before - something epic, something naughty! It was Christmas Eve night. Me, Matt and Daisy were feeling cheeky. Suddenly, one of the bricks on the chimney fell off - then another and another! All of a sudden, some old man came tumbling down the chimney! I got on my computer to look up who he was. Apparently, his name was Santa Claus. I found out that he gave children like me presents. I wanted to have *all* the gifts he had! Then Daisy had an idea...

"Aha!" she said. "I know how to get his gifts! Lock him in the shed and steal his sleigh!"

"Good idea!" exclaimed Matt.

Daisy took a gift and yelled, "Haha! Come and get me!"

Santa followed her into the small wooden shack. It was then when she realised she made a huge mistake! Santa had put his sleigh in the shed! Santa entered the small, tiny brown house and pulled a sword from his sleigh! Just as Daisy was about to be ended, Matt stepped in.

"Santa, since you do whatever kids want you to do... Get out of my shed and drop the sword!" he said.

Santa stepped away from Daisy.

"Haha!" Matt laughed. "Now give me the sword!"

And that's what Santa did. Suddenly, he jumped onto the sleigh, tapped a button and a squad of reindeer carried him away, leaving us absolutely nothing...

Oh, I forgot! He left his sword, but Daisy kept that. So this year, we got no Christmas presents!

Ellie Rose Makepeace (8)

St Benedict's RC Primary School, Ampleforth

The Incredible Diary Of... The Day I Lost My Ballet Shoe And Had A Show

Dear Diary,

What a week I've had!

Monday:

When I went to get the mail, I saw there was a letter addressed to me. When I opened the letter, I was shocked because it was for a ballet show in China and I only lived at Ampleforth! I had to tell my ballet teacher, so when I went the next day, she had a dance ready.

Tuesday:

When I woke the next morning, it was bright and fresh, so I had yoghurt and fruit with a sprinkle of cinnamon. After breakfast, I went upstairs to get ready for my ballet class.

After a long day at ballet, it was time to go home.

Wednesday:

This was my last practice, so I went to a different class that had a stage that looked like the stage in China. It was a late finish, but where was my ballet shoe?

Luckily, I found it four hours later - that was another long day!

Thursday:

I was on a plane, then it was time for my performance! That was the end of my week.

Grace Humpleby (8)

St Benedict's RC Primary School, Ampleforth

Paradise Dies!

Dear Diary,

Today was the worst/best/first day of my life. This morning, I woke up in paradise and I could hear my carrier talking so loud! She went on and on, so I decided to try and kick the wall down, but it didn't work. I felt furious!

Suddenly, a Big Mac fell onto my head. I couldn't wait to try it! I was starving - my last meal was ten minutes ago. I needed some McDonald's!

All of a sudden, at maybe 12:30pm, I found out that two and two equals twenty-two! Then I started to wonder, *will I live in paradise forever? And will I ever meet my carrier?*

Then I felt a rumble. It didn't sound good. Unexpectedly, I heard screams, and then my carrier said, "Get out!" so I started to panic.

When I thought all the madness had stopped, I saw light. I saw an amazing woman and her name was Mummy/Emma!

Daisy Naylor Smith (9)

St Benedict's RC Primary School, Ampleforth

The Incredible Diary Of... The Monster In School!

Dear Diary,

What a bad nightmare I've just had! I was in the car when, suddenly, I appeared in my old school in India! I was just standing there when, all at once, a monster jumped out at me. It scared the living daylights out of me!

He was all frothy and he was snarling. I thought he was going to chase me around - then I realised that the monster was getting my friend, Maroof Nadaf. I had to save him! Other people had already turned into monsters. What could I do?

I noticed that the firemen were hosing down people. I rushed and got a bucket of water. I turned to my friend and threw it at him. I was terrified and I couldn't believe that I'd actually done it! I quickly got more water to throw over the last monster. I did it, Diary!

Ryan Kambli (8)

St Benedict's RC Primary School, Ampleforth

The Incredible Diary Of... The Silly Dog

Dear Diary,

While I was sitting in my room, I did not know that the dog was in the kitchen eating wrapping paper! When I came in, the wrapping paper was empty! A few hours later, me and Mum went to walk the dog. When we got to the top of the hill, we stopped to look at a drain. We watched it for about ten minutes, then we walked a bit further. While we were on the hill, we thought we could make a camp. In our camp, we would have lots of yummy food. We got everything set up and got ready to go to sleep. My dog was sleeping with me - how exciting!

When I woke up, the dog had eaten all our food! Finally, we went home and my granny said, "I've got you a hamster!

"No!" I screamed.

Isaac Raynar (8)

St Benedict's RC Primary School, Ampleforth

The Incredible Diary Of... The Funny Moment

Dear Diary,

I have had a whale of a time after pushing a girl into my mud pit! I had never seen such a happy human fall in a mud pit ever before. When I saw her today, I already knew it would be a good day. When she came today, she was scattering food in the mud. Who would do such a thing? I decided I would push her over, so that's what I did. Since then, she has been crying. When she tried to get up, she slipped! Hahaha! What a fool she was. I still have the picture in my mind, then my good friend Bob came along and ate her hair. What a silly thing! *That's not grass*, I thought.

I will never forget this day, the funniest day of my life and one of my favourite days of my life yet!

Ernest Jones (9)

St Benedict's RC Primary School, Ampleforth

The Incredible Diary Of... The Day I Saved My Brother

Dear Diary,

It was the start of the summer holiday. My brother was out, trying to make Brian shut up because Caolin couldn't bear the noise that he was making, but he was only five - he didn't know what he was doing.

I went down the stairs (well, rolled down the stairs) and went to have my breakfast. Suddenly, my ears started to work and I heard a noise. It sounded like Brian or Caolin. It was happening in the hen pen, I thought.

I went outside and saw Caolin getting bitten by Brian! I was angry at this and ran as fast as my chubby, stubby legs could carry me to save my brother from Brian! I screamed while I was running round the garden, screaming after Brian to save Caolin from him.

Kaiden Daniel Baxter (9)

St Benedict's RC Primary School, Ampleforth

The Incredible Diary Of... The Cake Catastrophe

Dear Diary,

On Monday, I was happy as ever to be on this shimmering post outside near the car park. It was a lovely day, but there was so much noise from trucks, cars, trees swishing and people, as people kept throwing junk outside. I thought, *what would it be like to be fed by hand?*

I was eating peacefully until those birds started fighting - then I heard a noise, but it was only a silly car.

Uh-oh - people were coming towards me! One little person was going to feed me by hand! I grabbed the food out of her hand - but oh no! I couldn't breathe! I was choking!

I wondered if she would feed that to another bird. We will never know.

Finally, a vet came to pick me up.

Amelia Jasmin Syms (7)

St Benedict's RC Primary School, Ampleforth

The Incredible Diary Of... A Cockerel's Life

Dear Diary,

The day has been awful! It all started when the girls started to lay eggs everywhere. I was really annoyed!

Then she came in her big boots and giant coat with a scary grin. She opened the pen door and stared at me. I thought we were having a staring competition. I was getting really angry, so I walked towards her and started to peck her leg. She screamed. She picked up a twig and threw it at me. She turned around. Her grandma was standing there. She grabbed her by the arm and took her away. Phew! She was gone.

The day was over and I was settling down to go to sleep. That's when I heard screaming! I wondered who it could be...

Lexi Hillier (8)

St Benedict's RC Primary School, Ampleforth

The Incredible Diary Of... Cat Cat-Astrophe

Dear Diary,

This morning, I followed my owner into the bathroom and curled around her leg. She climbed into the white, wet bowl and I leapt onto the edge of the bowl and I started to shuffle along the side. I saw an oval-shaped pink thing and I slipped on it and slide down the side of the bowl! I wondered what would happen and, suddenly, I hit the water and I thought I was going to drown!

Then I felt two wet hands touch me and I jumped and bit the two hands! There was a scream and I heard the sound of booming feet rushing through the corridor. They opened the door, grabbed me and rubbed me with a rough blanket. I ran away...

Albert Nichols (7)

St Benedict's RC Primary School, Ampleforth

The Incredible Diary Of... A Finger Being Stuck In A Door

Dear Diary,

I'm still throbbing in pain whilst I write this. Today couldn't get any worse. My handler was fiddling with me and then it happened...

It all started when a tractor came to refill the hay. I saw it in the field. My handler was so excited to see the tractor - not so much me. He rushed to the door and placed me where the door would close. It started to creak, then *slam!* The pressure of the door made me furious and annoyed!

Once I had calmed down, it was a matter of getting to A&E. My handler was crying half of the way, then there was the injection...

Theodore Gabriel Carter (8)

St Benedict's RC Primary School, Ampleforth

The Incredible Diary Of... Climbing A Tree And Falling

Dear Diary,

This day couldn't be better! I was walking around and I saw a big tree and I decided to climb - then, when I was at the top, the branch I was holding broke and when it broke, I fell!

When I fell, I said, "Ah! My back!"

Then I started to cry. When I stopped crying, I said, "Mum, Dad! Help me, please!" and then they saw me and they helped me.

Then my parents told me not to climb that tree again in my life.

They said, "No iPad this week."

I will not forget this day in my life! This day was a bad day in my life.

Carlos Terricabras (9)

St Benedict's RC Primary School, Ampleforth

The Incredible Diary Of... The Big Escape!

Dear Diary,

My name is Eva, I'm an orphan and that's the worst thing about me. When I was only five, my parents died in a fire and I was sent to the most terrible orphanage. I tried to escape lots of times but never succeeded. I started to lose hope until today.

This morning, I woke up in the cold and icy dormitory. I sat up, slowly wrapping myself in the thin blanket on my bed to try and stay warm. Lilly (one of the younger girls) was crying in her pillow on the bed next to me. I called her name and she turned her head to look at me.

"Are you okay?" I asked.

Lilly wouldn't reply and just started sobbing more. At that moment, my deadly enemy, Shiela, and her best friend, Elizabeth, woke up.

"Oh Lilly, you're such a crybaby," groaned Shiela.

"Yeah, crybaby," repeated Elizabeth.

"I am not!" Lilly cried, still sobbing.

The other girls started waking up, groaning and shouting. Suddenly, we all heard someone thumping down the corridor and everyone scrambled back to bed, pulling the sheets over their heads. I grabbed Lilly and hugged her tight.

It was Miss Willman stomping and she shouted at everyone, saying she knew we were awake. She instructed us to get dressed, so we did and I got into my old-fashioned purple frock. We all had cold porridge for breakfast and then started on our chores.

I went and packed my things, planning to escape. As I crept downstairs, I heard a knock at the door. When I opened it, there was no one there. I decided that it was just one of the silly boys doing a knock and run. I was free! I scrambled around the city for the rest of the day.

Ella-May Chadwick (10)

The Michael Syddall CE (A) Primary School, Catterick Village

The Incredible Diary Of... Brave Unicorn

Dear Diary,

Yesterday was no ordinary day. It was the most exciting thing that ever happened to me. I went on a mystical adventure and I discovered that the pot of gold was missing at the end of the rainbow. However, a cheeky leprechaun stole the shiny gold to be rich.

It all started when I was walking in a magical forest then suddenly I saw a rainbow shining at the end of the forest so I followed it. When I got there, I saw a pot of gold. However, behind the large pot of gold was a small leprechaun. He giggled at me then the leprechaun snatched the gold right before my eyes then he ran away like nothing happened.

I investigated around the forest to solve the matter. Suddenly, a fairy flew up to me and guided me. I saw a few coins on the floor. I did think to myself, *I can track the leprechaun by following the coins on the floor!*

A few hours later, we crossed over at some talking trees giving us clues to where the leprechaun was. We kept on going until we were at the dangerous side of the forest. Nasty crocodiles waiting for lunch, slimy snakes on the trees, but the fairy was angry but anxious at the same time.

The fairy knew what to do. She made the crocodiles into friendly dolphins so we could get across. I felt scared for a moment. I could see the leprechaun sleeping so I asked the fairy if she could use her wand to make the gold fly over to us. She agreed. We cheered quietly.

We walked back to the village and gave all the poor people all the gold they needed. Me and the pink fairy were proud of ourselves so we said goodbye to each other.

Poppy Tallulah Levitt (10)

The Michael Syddall CE (A) Primary School, Catterick Village

The Incredible Diary Of... My Door Life

Dear Diary,

Ow, ow, ow! Again, again and again! I just can't stand this! I just wish we weren't in a town but in a nice, quiet area, not getting hit on the face by these annoying people. Every day, these people opening and closing me but when they close me, it's a big *smash!* Why am I made from metal? Then I see others that are prettier and when they see me they start to laugh! It makes me really sad. Do you know what the worst thing is? They coloured me in brown (with a marker, you'll see why). Upstairs, there's a pink door for Lucy, a blue door for Ben and for their parents, they have a yellow door. Lucy and Ben's parents always stare at me because I don't blend in with the colour of the room. How dare they!

One day, I heard that they said they were going to paint me white. I was so happy! Before I was placed into this house, I lived in Ikea and everybody was the same colour but in wood. I was the only door on my shelf, because the manager was seeing who would buy me. These people eventually bought me and they didn't understand why I was paint-proof. Wait, earlier, I said I was going to get painted.

No, my dreams have been crushed! I guess I will go back to the store, yay. I will see my friends again (if they are even there). Swing by tomorrow.

Libby Grace Sutherland (11)

The Michael Syddall CE (A) Primary School, Catterick Village

The Incredible Diary Of... The Snowflake

Dear Diary,

I know what you're thinking, but you're wrong. I was not created by Elsa, queen of Arendale. I was created by the cloud, not the one you get on your phone, the one in the sky. The mystical, magical sky. Although it kept me up there for ten days, what a waste!

When I finally fell from the sky, I got stuck on a ten-year-old girl's window for two days. Not once did she change out of her T-shirt and joggers, not even at night. As far as I am concerned, she just sat there and played on this thing called Fortnite. I thought that meant every two weeks!

When the wind peeled me painfully off that dreaded window, away from my new friend, Cornflake, I landed on this thing. I believe it is called a journey, or was it a travel? No, it was a car, or was it a motorcycle? My memory is very fuzzy at this moment in time. If only I were one of those new Samsung phones that get used all the time. I hear they're very popular now. Back to the journey, travel, car or motorcar. I landed on it just today and had a great time. There were other snowflakes with me but not as good friends as Cornflake.

Doesn't that sound like a double act? Snowflake and Cornflake. Anyway, we went to the pizza place. I'll write tomorrow, if I haven't melted.

Katie Proudlock (11)

The Michael Syddall CE (A) Primary School, Catterick Village

The Incredible Diary Of... Missing Mr Bear

Dear Diary,

Last week on Monday night, I could hardly even sleep, just like any other child who knew they were going to the airport as soon as they woke up. Our flight was at ten o'clock in the morning at Newcastle Airport. Me and my bear had never been on an aeroplane before, so I wasn't sure what it felt like.

When we had arrived at the airport, we had two hours to spare, so we went to the Burger King closest to us. My dad said it was a rip-off, but he's always like that when he's tired.

After eating and talking, we only had five minutes but our plane wasn't to be seen. Then, on a loudspeaker, we heard: "The ten o'clock flight to Tenerife is delayed for one and a half hours."

I was sure that was our flight and it really annoyed me because I was so excited to go.

An hour and a half boring hours passed by and we were boarding the ginormous plane. It was chaos for someone my age, especially because we were sat at the back of the plane. We got the snack trolley first though.

When the plane set off, it thudded and banged and that scared me, so I rumbled through my hand luggage but my teddy bear wasn't there! I suddenly remembered that it was at home on the sofa!

Max Lewis Coates (10)

The Michael Syddall CE (A) Primary School, Catterick Village

The Incredible Diary Of... Teddy!

Dear Diary,

I was loving my life until Toys 'R' Us got shut down. Now I am in Dave's corner shop! Like, don't get me wrong, I love it (I hate it) but no one comes into the shop.

Toys 'R' Us was magnificent because everyone, and I mean everyone, came in. It was so colourful and vibrant. I am Teddy. I know what you're thinking, I am not Mr Bean's teddy. Well, I wish I was! The workers always paid *most* of us respect. I say 'most' for a reason because they put me on the highest shelf in Toys 'R' Us, even though I am scared of heights but at least I didn't get slobbery hands all over me.

You don't want to know what Dave's unpopular corner shop is all about... All they sell is beans and toilet paper and one teddy - me. Being serious, I think they must have sent me to the wrong place. All of my other friends got sent to Smyth's Toys Superstores. I am annoying but am I that annoying for them to send me to Dave's corner shop? At least I've got Tim the toilet paper to talk to.

If you're reading this, please go to Dave's corner shop and buy me. I despise this place! Talk to you tomorrow, Teddy out!

Keira Stokell (11)

The Michael Syddall CE (A) Primary School, Catterick Village

The Incredible Diary Of... The Astronaut That Changed The World!

Dear Diary,

Today was amazing as I'd finally come back to Earth. Here's what happened. The head coordinator of NASA asked me to lead a mission to an undiscovered planet that was now on their radar. I wanted to go on the mission, but they didn't know what could have been on there. Was it dangerous?

I had to take the risk! A few days later, we boarded the rocket. The journey would take seven months! My nerves got the better of me at first, but I passed on.

After what seemed like years of eating pouched food, we arrived. It was colder than usual. We could finally explore! This planet was the size of the Earth with wildlife and animals too.

When it was dark, three moons were visible and were gazing onto the green blanket of grass. As we explored the jungle of life, we came across some civilisation, a type of village. We sprinted as the trees greeted us with joy, there were people... aliens! The most incredible thing was that they spoke English. We had to take one back, so we did.

170

After seven months more of eating pouched food, we made it back with the alien safely. They even named the planet after me: Violeta!

Izabel Violet Painter (10)
The Michael Syddall CE (A) Primary School, Catterick Village

The Incredible Diary Of... An Eco Ninja

Dear Diary,

Today, I was wandering around the neighbourhood when, suddenly, I saw some weeds running over to a human's garden! You may wonder how I saw them, well, I'm as big as an ant! Anyway, I was wondering what they were doing, so I tried to follow them.

I was too busy thinking about them that I forgot what garden they went into. Off I went through all the gardens. I finally got to number thirty-five. When I went in, it was too late. It was completely destroyed by the weeds.

I used the really long weed spray and it cured the garden. I started to think about cookies and I fell asleep. Low and behold, I woke up in a weed net. You may be wondering why I didn't use the spray. Well, I fell on the button and it all squirted out. It cured the whole garden permanently. I had saved Timmy's garden.

Suddenly, Timmy came outside. He leaned down and picked me up, "Hello there, what are you?"

"I am Eco Ninja, I have been protecting your garden!"

He answered, "Thank you!"
He then put me down and off I went to my happy little tree house.

Liam Martin (9)

The Michael Syddall CE (A) Primary School, Catterick Village

The Incredible Diary Of... Olly Orange

Dear Diary,

I've been sitting here for years (two days) and Mr Kiwi is making fun of my kind. Do you know what? When I'm popular, I'm gonna ban Mr Kiwi. Oh, where has he gone? No! He has been bought! I was ready to ban him from Tesco and put him in the free fruit basket. He was rotten.

If I get bought next, I will hop out the bag and follow Mr Kiwi. Then I shall ban him. But that can't happen because no one buys oranges anymore as kids nag that we're 'too orange' or 'too round' or worst of all 'they make me vomit'.

If I get eaten, I hope I'll turn into an awesome superfood: avocado.

Dear Diary,

Yes! I'm finally bought but I can't move! No! I'm filled up with fury and rage. Argh! I give up. I'll just sit in the fruit bowl and rot.

Dear Diary,

We're home and guess what? I'm in the fruit bowl rotting. I hate this. I just want to be a good food.

My left side has rotted and I'm going in the bin.
But you see, cruel world, this isn't the last of me!

Riley Lister (10)

The Michael Syddall CE (A) Primary School, Catterick Village

The Incredible Diary Of... Me And My Hoover

Dear Diary,

Yesterday, I was playing with my football but then, my mum shouted, "Lauren, go and hoover your room!"

I thought, *I never hoover my room*, and I went down the stairs to get the hoover. It was so heavy. When I got to my room, I started to hoover but suddenly, the hoover went out of control.

"Oh no! Oh no! Mum!" I exclaimed, but she didn't answer.

That same day, I got the Hoover to stop. I left the hoover on the landing but somehow, it turned back on.

"No, not again!" I cried out. "Why?"

The hoover went all the way downstairs and outside. It went all the way down the street, bumping into people, causing chaos.

"Sorry! It's out of control!"

No one believed me.

As it slowed down, one of the men walked past and the Hoover bumped into him. He luckily stopped it.

"Thank you! Thank you!" I said, out of breath. Suddenly, the town went all quiet and it went back to normal. Everyone was relieved, after all, that man saved the Hoover.

Lauren Emily Freer (9)

The Michael Syddall CE (A) Primary School, Catterick Village

The Incredible Diary Of... Pauline The Potato

Dear Diary,

It's lonely, it's dark and the last thing I had remembered was being a seedling, getting planted into the ground by an old, wrinkly man (his house stank!).

Once I said that, a metal object went into the mud next to me and lifted me up. I thought I was free but all I saw was the same wrinkly man but he had more wrinkles.

He brought me inside with his old-man hands and put me on a kitchen table. It smelt like old people but the last time I was there, it smelt like a toe mixed with a muddy pig. This time, I could see with my eyes the whole kitchen. I was in a basket and next to is was Paul! All crispy and cooked! I panicked because the oldie was coming to the kitchen and I thought he was going to cook me but he picked me up and put me in a pot with boiling water.

"Mayday! Mayday! This is the end!"

I wish I was treated nicely. Spuds aren't supposed to be like this, right?

Wait, how am I alive? Meh. Okay, it's not too bad. I might get eaten soon so see you in your next packet of crisps!

Phoebe Barnard (10)

The Michael Syddall CE (A) Primary School, Catterick Village

The Incredible Diary Of... Billy The Boring Clock

Dear Diary,

I am really getting sick of this! Ever since I was bought from that unpopular shop full of old, broken tat, all I have ever heard is *tick-tick-tock.* My uneven arms (which can get very annoying) are getting really stiff and I am always really tired. Well, that's not surprising, I have to work 24/7 (literally) with no break. Every morning, I get vibrated with a big, loud ring and then a big sort of creature which took me away from that shop starts groaning! Then I'm like, "Please, woman (or man, I'm not sure), at least you get a break!"

Then, something terrible happened. My tick, it was gone! My arms, they weren't moving! My first break after five million years! Wait, what was happening? I was flying! A big stick thing was poked into me and that long, thick and chilly thing went into my back.

Well, here we are again, back with ticking, morning vibrations, uneven arms and a groaning creature. Until next time, Billy the boring clock.

Francesca Rouse (10)

The Michael Syddall CE (A) Primary School, Catterick Village

Dog's Diary

Dear Diary,

Do you know what? I'm getting sick of this. I'm getting told off for picking up shoes but I get wound up by the cat. They're like, "Get out the blinds! Stop picking up shoes!"

Nag, nag, nag.

"Stop doing that! Get down off the sofa!"

Ever since I have been born, I have been bumping into the doors. Why can't they keep the doors open? I headbutt them all the time. It hurts my head but how else am I supposed to get there attention? I have not got any hands. I go on walks but they take a ball, like come on! They throw, I chase after it but then they're like, "Drop!"

But it is my ball so I don't give it back. They all come down in their pyjamas at 6am. I was so tired. I wish they would let me on the sofa and let me sleep with a blanket and a teddy. At least they give me hugs and kisses. I wish I was a cat. At least I could get some peace, and I would be able to wind up dogs. Yours sincerely, Bailey.

Lexie Hurst (10)

The Michael Syddall CE (A) Primary School, Catterick Village

The Adventure Of Booky

Dear Diary,

Hi, my name is Booky. A few days ago was one of the worst, most horrible days of my life. Things did get better. First, I'll tell you about myself: I have one eye, a purple mouth, a red, square head, a long, blue, square body. I also have red stick arms, green stick legs and last but not least, I have a bright red diamond heart.

When my maker (Lucy) and her parents go to sleep, I like to explore. My first time exploring, I got lost. I ended up in this big room with a TV in and lots of furniture and pictures all around. I was so scared, I just started crying.

I cried for thirty seconds and then, a bear came up to me. I was freaking out, I thought my head was going to explode. It looked nice and friendly.

I asked, "What's your name?"

She replied, "My name is Buttercup. What's yours?"

The bear was nice and fluffy, its fur was snow-white and now, me and Buttercup are best friends.

Lucy-Mai Fotheringham (10)

The Michael Syddall CE (A) Primary School, Catterick Village

The Incredible Diary Of...

Dear Diary,

I'm sick of being a hairy kiwi in this house. I have been in the fruit bowl for a year. All my owner does is nag, nag, nag and all she calls me is a hairy sour blob and I am sick of the orange next to me. Whenever I try to speak, all he does is laugh. He is exactly like the annoying orange because he is an orange and annoying. Before my fat owner was a vegan, all she did was eat McDonald's. I had lots of friends but now I have no friends because she ate them all with a spoon. I had lots of friends but now I have no one because she ate them all with a spoon! If she doesn't eat the orange next to me or me, I'm going to eat her with a spoon! Oh, and I can't forget about Apple Adam. All he does is insult me. Yesterday, he called me a green, hairy, fat-headed blob and every time I call him something, all he says back is, "At least I'm not green inside!" Little does he know, I am going to eat him next...

Jack Anthony Buttitta (11)

The Michael Syddall CE (A) Primary School, Catterick Village

The Adventure Of Dog Thing Trigger

Dear Diary,

The first thing that ever happened to me when I, Trigger, was born, the vet said, "What is that?" Then I started to headbutt my mother. After six weeks of torture, I was abducted by a hobgoblin and a garden gnome. To be honest, I'm glad I'm not getting pillows lobbed at me anymore

As soon as I got to my 'forever home', the first thing I wanted to do was have a wee on the sofa. As I was weeing, all I saw was a big, brown object advance around the house which was my doggy brother, Rodney.

After my training, and a few concussions, I was ready to go on my first walk which was the same as most where I had to stay on the lead because my owner thought I would headbutt another animal or thing.

Then, when I was all trained, I could headbutt anything like toilets, radiators, doors, people, chairs and beds. Luckily, I am not as dumb now. Well, see you tomorrow, Diary.

Stanton Sharkey (11)

The Michael Syddall CE (A) Primary School, Catterick Village

The Incredible Diary Of... Me And My Dog!

Dear Diary,

Eight years ago, I was just playing with my dog in the living room. Then suddenly, I heard a noise. "Liam! Liam!"

It was getting louder and louder. It was too quiet to be my sister or my mum or dad, so I went around the house, asking people if they'd said my name. They all said no. I even asked my three cats. They meowed like usual, so I meowed back.

Later that day, I heard someone say my name again. This time, I went to my dog. I asked him if he knew who said my name and he said, "Yes, it was me."

I fainted, then woke up.

On the sofa next to me was my dog saying, "Liam! Liam! Wake up! Wake up!"

I fainted again and woke up. Then I started taking him on walks. I asked him if other people could hear him, he said, "No, because I share some DNA with you. I'm only joking. Anyone can hear me."

We became best friends.

Liam Townley (9)
The Michael Syddall CE (A) Primary School, Catterick Village

The Incredible Diary Of... The Lost Puppy

Dear Diary,

One day, I was playing outside and when I came inside, I got my shoes off and went to get Puggo. I couldn't find her so I looked outside, in the downstairs bathroom, the living room, my mum's room, the upstairs toilet and the playroom. We couldn't find her. I started crying, I couldn't sleep without that dog.

We looked under my quilt and there was Puggo! I was so happy. I jumped around and, when I woke up the next morning, Puggo was asleep. I woke her up and I got her a drink and food. She had her breakfast and drank her water, then we woke up my mum. We all took Puggo for a walk.

We went home and had dinner. I played outside and then, I went inside for tea and went to play for ten more minutes with Puggo.

Casey Ann Pickup (9)

The Michael Syddall CE (A) Primary School, Catterick Village

The Incredible Diary Of... Harry And His Weekend

Dear Diary,

This weekend, me, my dad and my sister went to the Foxglove Nature Resort and I saw three deer, although Dad and Elena only saw two. After that, we went to the lovely, wonderful restaurant in Catterick Garrison. Then we stayed in our house and I went on Fortnite while Dad and Elena had naps. Our mum was at her dad's.

On Sunday, we had a wonderful treat and Dad took us to Vue cinemas to see 'The Kid Who Would Be King'. It is based on King Arthur and his sister's battle. Then, after that, we went to Pizza Hut for tea and that was in Darlington.

After that, we went home and then, Mum came home too. I then went back on Fortnite and, at bedtime, I read 'Grandpa's Great Escape' to my mum.

Harry Hooson (10)

The Michael Syddall CE (A) Primary School, Catterick Village

The Adventures Of Luna The Cat

Dear Diary,

My year has been tragic. My owners keep going out and forgetting me, which is despicable. When they go out, they forget to feed me, so I get left alone with no food and no protection from my nemesis, the sofa.

I scratch it and it shouts, "Luna!"

That might actually be my oldest owner.

When my owners return, the youngest (Justin) has fun with me as I lie on him and he strokes me but, when I get comfortable, three enemies arise: his brother, the stairs and the mattress.

Today, I wondered if I belonged here and who knew. I just wanted food, I didn't care what the boy, the teenager and the mother were doing.

Justin Burgess (10)

The Michael Syddall CE (A) Primary School, Catterick Village

The Incredible Diary Of...

Dear Diary,

A few days ago, my mum and dad said that they would take me to the outside world: the rainforest in Brazil! When I walked through the magic door. I was shocked because there were lots of animals about. We travelled along the water slowly. I was full of excitement. We visited toy shops and had fun.

Mum and Dad said, "One day, you can tell your children and visit again."

I thought and asked if we could go back the next day. We all hopped back on the boat and went through the water.

Today, I found out that my parents owned the rainforest, the animals were full of joy and so was I!

Boe Kirk (10)

The Michael Syddall CE (A) Primary School, Catterick Village

The Incredible Diary Of... The Rage On Fortnite

Dear Diary,

Today, I have faced many emotions like anger, defeat, pain and annoyance. I have only gotten one win today, that's it! Not long ago, I was throwing my Xbox controller around the room and I was screaming my head off over me dying on Fortnite.

I'm starting to think that everyone is too good now that season eight has come out. I'm not saying I'm a noob or anything, but there are so many pro players out there like Ninja, Ali-A and many more. If Fortnite does not get easier by tomorrow, I will change to Apex Legends.

Lewis Bell (9)

The Michael Syddall CE (A) Primary School, Catterick Village

The Incredible Diary Of... The Attic Monster

Dear Diary,

On Friday, I slept at my auntie's and she said, "Get me some logs for the fire. They're in the attic." When I went to get some logs, she locked me in! I was scared because I had heard of the attic monster that lived in her attic and it would eat you up with one big gulp. I saw some eyes...

"Argh!" I said, switching the light on to see a big, ugly, hairy monster with razor-sharp teeth. "Don't eat me!" I said, terrified.

Instead, it went to the back of the attic, scared, and it started crying.

I asked if it was okay and it said, "Nobody likes me. I just want a friend."

I said, "You can be my friend."

I hugged the monster. After an hour or so, I heard the door open and I said to the monster, "I'd better go. Bye."

I waved to the monster as I left.

"Who were you talking to?" asked my auntie.

"Nobody," I said, smiling.

Chloe Gibson (9)

Thomas Hinderwell Primary Academy, Scarborough

191

The Incredible Diary Of...
Captain Pug

Dear Diary,

Today, I travelled the seas. I stopped to have a delicious lunch break. After my lunch, I had a little roam around the island and I came across a bunch of chests and crates. As I got closer to examine my find, I saw parts of a ship floating on the surface of the sea. One of the chests was open and I could see some extravagant-looking jewellery seeping over the edge.

I decided to explore the waters. I dived into the ocean and swam deep down to the bottom of the sea. It was a sight of sheer beauty. The coral reefs were elegant like fine art shimmering in the moonlight. As I swam further, I came across the finest, most exquisite vessel I had ever seen. I swam to the vessel and looked through a porthole. Inside, it was just as gorgeous as the outside with fine, mahogany trims and pearlescent tiles.

I decided that I wanted this ship as my own, so I swam to shore to retrieve my ship and embarked on the task of bringing the vessel to shore. Once ashore, I cleaned the vessel and restored her to her former glory. I decided to use this vessel as a place to call home.

I heaved the treasure and the crates aboard my newfound home and tied my ship to the shoreline. As I stood admiring my new home, I realised that I suddenly had an island to call my own. Needing a name for this island, I racked my brains and decided I would call it Scarborough Bay.
What a day! I found a new home, acquired an island and became the richest pirate in one day!

Kyle Charlie Smith (11)
Thomas Hinderwell Primary Academy, Scarborough

The Incredible Diary Of... The Long Adventure

Dear Diary,

One Saturday, together with my parents and grandmother, we decided to go for a hike in a nearby town. On the way, we could see fields full of sheep and bunnies and grass that was very dense. This sight gave me feelings of nostalgia but, at the same time, joy because it resembled my native country.

Getting to the town, we stopped in a park, but it was unfortunately closed. There was a very nice restaurant with a children's area. It had a lake and a large swimming pool too!

Defeated by the beauty of the restaurant, we decided to go in for lunch. The waitress greeted us nicely and the service was great. In terms of the food, I can say it was delicious and very tasty. Shortly after, we resumed our hike until we arrived at a very beautiful and green forest full of coloured flowers with a river and more lakes. In the middle of the forest, there was a beautiful church and a beautiful garden. It was a dream landscape.

The pheasants and bunnies were floating among the trees and the birds were singing a very cheerful song.

Because it was late, we decided to go home, but get back through the forest as quickly as possible. After the hike, we had a feeling of joy because we saw new places, met new people and at the same time, this hike made me feel a sense of nostalgia because it resembled my birthplace and where I grew up.

Andreas Nikolos Neagoe (10)

Thomas Hinderwell Primary Academy, Scarborough

The Life Of A Farmer

Dear Diary,

Today has been an extremely busy day. I woke up at 5:30am to a sheep in high distress. A lamb was almost dead, buried deep in the straw and what looked to be a bunch of lambs on the way. I tried to deliver them myself, however, they were tangled together. It was a job for the vet.

Whilst the vets were on their way, I began to try and breathe life into the first lamb. First, I cleared his airways by poking a straw into his nostrils, but that didn't work. Then I tried massaging his lungs, but there was no hope, it was dead!

As soon as the vets arrived, they did an emergency caesarian section. First, the vets had to shave the sheep, then they had to inject some pain relief into the area to numb it. Next, they made the incision into the skin. The vets began to remove the lambs, one at a time.

I started to breathe life into one, but the third one didn't make it. Well, that's what I thought.

Finally, the vets sewed up the sheep and began to pack up and leave when the third lamb started to move its head up and down and make a squeaky noise. It was alive!

I put all three of them into a pen and turned on a heat lamp to keep them warm. I finally went home to celebrate the birth of three healthy lambs.

Lily Sellers (11)
Thomas Hinderwell Primary Academy, Scarborough

The Incredible Diary Of...A Gymnastics Competition

Dear Diary,

Hi, I am Daisy and I had a gymnastics competition today. It was my first competition, I needed to wear a leotard and silk leggings. I needed my hair in a bun with a shiny pink bobble.

I got in the car and we went. There were a lot of people there. I went inside the gym to warm up. Then the adults came in and we performed our routine.

I did front somersaults on a trampette. I did a pike as well. There was quite a lot of people performing. There were hundreds of people watching us.

We put in a lot of work to get this far. We all acted like professionals doing it.

At the end, Megan, Joseph and Damian did fantastic tricks on tumble. Megan added a backwards roll because she nearly fell.

After that we did medals and my group came third which is a bronze medal. We were really pleased with ourselves.

I went home really pleased.

Daisy Grace Clayton (8)

Thomas Hinderwell Primary Academy, Scarborough

The Incredible Diary Of... Oliver The Explorer

Dear Diary,

I went on an adventure to ancient Egypt. It all started when I was wandering across the street and found a mysterious object lying on the ground. It appeared to be a portal-creator and I was sucked into a portal.

I landed inside a pyramid and I saw a person that appeared to be wearing toilet paper all over them. It was a mummy! I touched it and its eyes opened. It was holding a short, dark knife. It started to charge. A portal appeared and I jumped in. It closed just in time.

I landed next to the Roman army. I ran into the blacksmiths, the blacksmith was holding the object that had created the portal that took me to ancient Egypt! I grabbed it and a portal opened. It took me back home.

At first, I thought that it was just a dream, but when I found the object in my pocket, I chucked it out the window and went to bed.

Oliver Gough (7)

Thomas Hinderwell Primary Academy, Scarborough

The Incredible Diary Of...

Dear Diary,

Today, Dad and I went to the swimming pool. We went down the slides and it made me happy and excited. It was really fast and fun. We had a nice day there. We travelled to the pool by bus and I paid the driver and got a ticket. On the way there, it started raining, but we had our coats with us, so we didn't get wet.

We stayed at the pool for a long time. We had lots of fun.

Mason Tindall (9)

Thomas Hinderwell Primary Academy, Scarborough

YoungWriters® Est. 1991

Young Writers Information

We hope you have enjoyed reading this book – and that you will continue to in the coming years.

If you're a young writer who enjoys reading and creative writing, or the parent of an enthusiastic poet or story writer, do visit our website **www.youngwriters.co.uk**. Here you will find free competitions, workshops and games, as well as recommended reads, a poetry glossary and our blog. There's lots to keep budding writers motivated to write!

If you would like to order further copies of this book, or any of our other titles, then please give us a call or order via your online account.

Young Writers
Remus House
Coltsfoot Drive
Peterborough
PE2 9BF
(01733) 890066
info@youngwriters.co.uk

Join in the conversation!
Tips, news, giveaways and much more!

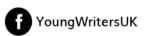 YoungWritersUK    @YoungWritersCW